Also by Louis Begley

WARTIME LIES

THE MAN WHO WAS LATE

Louis Begley

THE

MAN

WHO

WAS

LATE

Alfred A. Knopf   New York   1993

for Anka

THE MAN WHO WAS LATE

I

IT WAS A PARADOX, of which Ben over the years became fond, that he, ostensibly the most punctual and reliable of men, should have been late in the major matters of existence, that he always somehow missed his train. For all that the world could see, his comings and goings were meticulously planned and executed; he could be counted on to leave and arrive unfailingly, and precisely at the appointed hour—whatever his destination. But he knew better. Having studied to death his own version of the universal timetable, he discovered that somehow everything had been timed wrong, had been botched. Ben elaborated on his theory over countless lunches with me. Provided he was in New York, and the peripeties of some financial combination of the decade he just happened to be bringing to the desired ending did not interfere—the pages of my desk calendar were most often blank—we met for lunch at least once a month. Sometimes, if the conversation seemed unfinished—because what we had meant to say could not be contained in the conventional space of two hours, or because we were interrupted by an intruder determined to catch up with one or the other of us, insensitive to the bored or disparaging banter with which, in our mood of conniving solidarity, we deflected his questions—we would agree to lunch again the very first day he was free, to make sure the thing was finally talked out. This was our habit during almost fifteen years. For Ben, after completing the rites of passage proposed to the nation's best during the Eisenhower era—Harvard College, followed by service in the marines, travel in Europe on a famed scholarship—moved to New York.

By then, I had been living here for several years, ever since my own graduation three classes ahead of Ben, enjoying a precocious celebrity due to a short novel I had published at the midpoint between the appearance of *The Old Man and the Sea* and *Goodbye, Columbus*. It was based loosely on a shipwreck off Point Judith in which my older brother, the war hero, had drowned. The accident happened on a Thanksgiving weekend while I was still at school—in fact on restriction. Neither his body nor that of the friend who had come along as crew was found. After a week's search by the Coast Guard, and planes chartered by my parents, someone retrieved objects from their boat: a couple of life preservers, my brother's Bible in a pink rubber sack, miscellaneous navigation gadgets. Father paid our school to accept the gift of Sam's books and keep them, together with a watercolor portrait of him as a Navy flyer, in a corner of the library. Then he and my mother carried on as though nothing had changed in their lives. My book was a success with critics and the public. Many heard in it echoes of Melville and Crane; a reviewer's concluding line, that I had "set down the postwar generation's theodicy," was taken seriously and repeated in interviews and profiles, although nothing of the sort had crossed my mind. Until I decided that I must write this story,

I did not undertake any other work of imagination. There was no subject that engaged me sufficiently.

Whether Ben and I had met in Cambridge was a question we never resolved. If, as Ben claimed, some encounter had occurred—this was the sort of detail about which my otherwise precise friend was sometimes vague or wrong—it left no mark on my memory. So far as I know, our friendship began at the New York dinner table of a classmate of Ben's who worked for the same magazine as I. Ben was then married to Rachel. They gave parties at their Park Avenue spread with a frequency and nonchalance the rest of us gaped at with more than a tinge of envy. All the while, as Ben later told me, they were inside their marriage like birds caught in some high-ceilinged room: confused, crashing into walls and closed windows, searching for an opening, for a long time unable to get out. Because my own wife and I came to dislike Rachel's knack for putting Ben down before their guests— she was unendingly talkative and witty—our relationship changed from a friendship of two couples into a friendship of two men who lunch together. The wives, tacitly excluded, assumed the role of that sort of former friend one greets at large gatherings with five minutes of concentrated flattery and then abandons, hands raised in a gesture of ambiguous benediction.

Paradoxes and other conceits invented by Ben lent a thematic continuity to our conversations. Without Rachel there to contradict him, he talked well, listening to his own words with just enough satisfaction to amuse me when I caught him at it. Like Conrad's Marlow, that exemplary *auteur manqué*, he preferred that the shape of his meaning emerge slowly, as though from concentric circles of a metaphor. Speaking too well, seeking to impose order on casual noontime chatter, were in fact among the defects and virtues that Ben and I shared. I would occasionally point out to Ben these ways in which we might be thought to be alike, whereupon he at once referred enthusiastically to other similarities, not all of which I was glad he had perceived. Physically, we did not resemble each other at all. Ben looked to me Hungarian (which he was not): by the standards of his Harvard friends, on the small side, nimble and compact, with thick brown hair of great vivacity. His ears, paper thin, stuck out. I was almost a head taller, blond at that time, with features and heft bequeathed by my Yorkshire and German ancestors. And I liked Ben, had liked him from the start, and had watched my affection for him grow with a mixture of self-approval and amusement. That his oddness and the touch of the exotic about him didn't put me off, that instead these qualities drew me to him like a magnet, proved some theories I held and had been heard to espouse about my people's traditions.

To return to Ben's sense of irremediable existential tardiness, the truth is that, until shortly before the events that brought his life to a tragic close, I did not take it seriously; in fact, I used to think that the only time Ben had missed his boat or train was when he did not make an effort to become a writer. Instead, flabbergasting and disappointing the intellectuals among his classmates, the teachers long accustomed to write recommendations for him, and perhaps even Rachel, although she claimed credit for Ben's decision, he went to work for a Wall Street investment bank that was both power-ful and impeccably elegant.

According to Ben, only his mother and father were not astonished, in part because they did not fully measure the droll uniqueness of finding a postwar refugee from Central Europe within those precincts, and in part because they had come to assume that Ben would always get what he wanted and that he would naturally want whatever put the greatest distance between them and him. As to Ben's real motives, he agreed with my assessment: he had as usual been, at least on the surface, unbeatably punctual in taking care that his obligations were met. He had promised to have a career that corresponded to Rachel's notion of living in the great world; such a career was now open to him. He badly needed money of his own; he would earn it. Without money, he foresaw a bleak future of dependence on Rachel's income to lift him and her above quotidian mediocrity and the sting of not being able to supplement the income of those spurned and confused parents. But, if he succeeded, if he came to have money in abundance, those oppressive problems would disappear. What's more, he would have arranged things so that his tasks would henceforth be set for him by others—first by the bank's partners, those wonderfully tailored men crossing and uncrossing their long legs under photographs of their sail-boats, and, later, by clients. Then it would not be necessary, in order to win his bread and whatever he wanted to spread on it, to do much rummaging in the rag-and-bone shop of the heart. According to Ben, he wished to avoid that activity at almost any cost; he didn't like what he found there.

It was therefore only logical, he would explain, that he should become his grand bank's house Jew—but whenever it was that he formed this view of his employment, he did not express it until some years later, after they had made him a partner, once again exactly on time according to the schedule governing such matters. This happened in the year that man first floated free in space, a coincidence that Ben alluded to as both suitable and pleasant. But in other respects, for Ben, his orderly ascension was just an additional illustration of how he would arrive on the platform, panting, beginnings of sweat breaking on his brow, after the train had left: for by that time, his parents had died without seeing how well he had done, how amply he intended to include them in his prosperity, and Rachel's views no longer mattered in any positive sense. She had thrown him over. The thought that his manifest success might add to the sum of her regrets was sweet; it was also unworthy.

Ben rarely mentioned these grimmer aspects of not being on time. He had a store of other illustrations that permitted him to spin out the theory and have others join in tolerant laughter at his expense without unduly obscuring the more satisfactory aspects of his career. Indeed, each anecdote of supposed failure could also be taken for a milestone of his progress.

Take Ben's clothes. God only knows what he wore before Rachel took him in hand: judging from a photograph or two I have seen of him at Harvard, it was boxy, pseudo-tweed creations "of good quality," draped self-consciously, as though the wearer suffered from an intermittent itch, over white shirts, and the wrong sort of old-man neckties. The photographs do not reveal his legs or feet, but one can imagine brown trousers and laced shoes acquired at Florsheim's. At a time when *The Catcher in the Rye* was becoming a manual of approved conduct, and the minutiae of preppy costume made or unmade a man with some finality, such attire would have sufficed—even without Ben's browner-than-usual hair combed back unparted and shaved high over the neck and ears—to mark him as a turkey: the Widmerpool of Harvard Yard. Much of this was, of course, more or less repaired by the time the Park Avenue dinners started. From foot to crown, Ben was accoutred in Brooks Brothers standard issue, except for certain details implying an even higher level. These included striking Florentine neckties procured by Rachel (until she decided that the attention she paid to Ben's appearance was demeaning to her and inconveniently likely to add to his growing self-esteem), brown English shoes that he wore to the office, against Wall Street rules, and also in the evening— homage to Rachel's unproved Bostonian theory that American gentlemen avoid black footwear—and perhaps the first Tyrolean loden coat to appear on the back of a Park Avenue resident.

As Ben began to take modest steps toward prosperity, his continuing and acute observation of the world, and of his own image in every available mirror, revealed the imperfections of the Brooks style: trousers too long in the crotch and dismally flapping about the ankles when they should have gracefully broken over the shoe; the middle button in a suit coat placed less than an inch below the sternum; the disgrace of a vent that, resisting all home remedies—safety pins, stitches secretly added at the top by his own hand to fasten the damn thing in place—refused to remain closed and instead spread revealingly over the wearer's buttocks. The litany of these small tragedies was long. They brought him to search for a tailor, a search he conducted in Paris, where his work increasingly took him, in preference to London.

He confessed to me that the inconvenience of having fittings in a city he visited rarely was only a part of the reason: he was not quite ready for a Savile Row silhouette; Rachel would have teased him mercilessly; according to her dictum, he was not "white" enough to be stylish. He could justify a Paris suit on the grounds of wanting clothes that fit him specifically, and not each and every white-collar operative of roughly similar dimensions, and that, if he found the right maker, would look mystifyingly American, although of finer quality and fabrication. At least, that's how he imagined it and that is how, after much study of guidebooks and gossip, he stumbled into the establishment of Monsieur Jeanne, an improbably named, French-speaking English tailor established in a shop on the avenue de l'Opéra.

There, the books were kept and the advance, before credit could be established, was demanded by Monsieur Jeanne's equally English wife; bolts of the heaviest English woolens lay on mahogany tables; on the walls were pictures of General de Gaulle and Guy de Rothschild, and also of lesser luminaries, with affectionate dedications to the man with a golden thimble. The General, according to Monsieur Jeanne, had used him for everything before he came to power, the Baron only for corduroy britches of a quality so superb that they could not be worn out. Indeed, the orders eventually stopped; the Baron would never need another pair. It hardly mattered: Monsieur Jeanne was liquidating his stock. There was a *gentilhommière* near Poitiers where he and "la Mrs.," as he called her, were spending more and more time, and where they would retire.

Monsieur Jeanne recognized Ben for the opportunity he was—unnaturally polite, seemingly indifferent to prices but terrified inside by the expense, ripe for trousers with "kidney warmers" climbing up the back, voluminous and admirably sewn—more unattributable and unrecognizable than Ben could have imagined. The only sore point was that, if they were totally different from their Brooks Brothers predecessors, they were also even more misshapen, requiring repeat visits to Monsieur Jeanne, which took most of Ben's free time in Paris, prevented him from traveling light, put him in danger of missing airplane connections while he waited for his luggage to appear. Inside the suitcases were Monsieur Jeanne's "patients": on the way to Paris, this meant garments in need of surgery; their cousins traveled to New York for a test of the extent of their recovery. According to Ben, the operations Monsieur Jeanne undertook were like Peter Lorre's work on Boris Karloff in *Arsenic and Old Lace*: the monstrousness of his creations increased with each session. All of this, Ben assured me—failure, waste of time, and expense—could be explained by bad timing. He had gone to a great tailor but had arrived late, after the tailor's illustrious clients had left him for some other *faiseur* unknown to Ben. The bloom was off the rose.

Ben's repertory of misadventures of this sort at times seemed inexhaustible; fortunately, it was also eclectic. Item: A great comic playwright, recently transformed into a French

academician, vacationing for the first time in Maine, be-
friended Ben. Together, they filled long and intimate evenings with gossip about Oriane and Baron de Charlus. The
master's praise of Ben's memory and penetration were un-
stinting—even Rachel was momentarily silenced—but the
master had decided he would never write again and was
drinking as heavily and methodically as when he was at the
height of his powers. How preponderant then were loneliness, and the wine and scotch that Ben dispensed, in the
scales of friendship, even assuming, as Ben must, that the old
man was somewhat glad to talk about Proust in his own
language in the Protestant wilderness of a Penobscot Bay
island—why else would he have trudged, day after day,
across the wide, overgrown meadow to be, as he said, *du côté
de chez Ben*? And why make a pretense of friendship when
his power to terrorize hosts and guests and to dominate
conversation seemed intact? How urgent, on the other hand,
was the need to provide those regular feasts of lobster and
corn, consumed in the company of the local gentry, for the
wife who looked and talked like a pastry-shop cashier and
for the spinster daughter who talked like the Communist high
school teacher she really was?

It was too bad to ask these questions, Ben complained.
Had Rachel's friends only lent the master their summerhouse
five years sooner, when he was writing his last play, there
would have been no room for such debasing ambiguity and,
besides, might not at least one of the endless discourses he
had listened to been redeemed by an epiphany? But who
could say that the master would have chosen him as a vacation friend in those earlier times? Ben thought it was far from

clear. When the playwright was still writing, he might not have had the time to spend with the young banker and his rich and elegant wife and his stepchildren (or the inclination to do so), whatever they put on the table or poured into a glass. He would have been instead conversing—in baby French and broken English or, as a last resort, through the pedant daughter—with those same producers, actors, and directors who later abandoned him when his star set, going off to lionize other men of genius as yet unknown to Ben, about money and professional subjects to which Ben and Rachel could contribute nothing. After the summer ended, Ben wrote several letters to the master, only the first of which was answered. And, having told once or twice too often the story of this encounter with greatness that had come too late, Ben never dialed the playwright's unlisted telephone number when he was in Paris and never knocked on the door of the apartment on the boulevard Raspail, although the temptation came upon him each time he passed under its oval balcony.

To top it all, there was the matter of Rachel, which I believe he discussed only with me. I really cannot think whom else he would have taken into his confidence. Was it not there that he missed the chance of all chances, the prize sweeter than any other, the bliss of being loved by her? And was not that too a case of being late, arriving after others had raided the pantry of her affections and had left, in place of the sweet honey he craved, only the smudgy marks of their frequent passage? These older, well-traveled, and confident men (such, at least, were the ones Rachel named: such had been her late husband) seemed to have been pedagogues of merit. Not content to "show her the ropes"—Rachel's own colloquial expression, Ben assured me—so that there was no gesture or inclination of the body an occasion might call for that she had not already experienced and memorized, had they not also formed her taste in drink, books, and clothes, taught her the names of hotels to avoid in the principal capitals, walked at her side down the galleries of the museums where she in turn guided Ben's novice gaze? The late husband had fathered Sarah and Rebecca, her queerly named, dangerously black-haired twins, and then was electrocuted in the course of some complex repair he was attempting to perform on the roof of his barn. Rachel was still in mourning, was actually dressed in black—a violation of Cambridge mores, but how could she forgo the thrilling contrast that widow's weeds made with her improbably white, impeccable skin?—when they met at the home of a Bostonian classmate. In Ben's freshman year, of the large-boned adolescents who mysteriously all knew one another, knew all the prettier girls at Radcliffe, and attended club punches, this curly-haired hockey player alone had manifested considerable and benevolent interest in his strange fellow student who talked like a book and seemed to know nobody. Ben was seated beside Rachel at the table; his eyes could not leave her creamy, lightly powdered cleavage. He was a drowning man; another moment, and he would plunge his face into it. His sentimental and worldly education were about to begin: Was not his tutor, mistress, and wife-to-be asking, at the end of lunch, whether he wanted to see her two-year-old girls, and did he really know fairy tales by heart, and would he come the next day to tea?

Toward the end of Ben's sophomore year, Rachel's widowed father died. There were no brothers or sisters to share in the cornucopia of terminating trusts. The dollar was strong. Rachel took a large house outside Hyères for the summer— Edith Wharton's former presence affecting the choice—and invited Ben to join her. A Harvard scholarship student to take care of the twins was just the thing; he would be like an older brother and supply the masculine presence needed for their correct development. She would pay his passage and a small salary. That there should be a salary confused Ben's parents sufficiently about their son's relations with the worrisome older woman from Boston. They gave their consent; Ben believed he must have it.

The house was, in the custom of that place, romantically dilapidated. Through the garden and a grove of parasol pines that prolonged it, one reached a shallow white beach. That is where, in the morning and also in the afternoon, after they had finished their long nap, Ben led the twins, rubbed suntan oil into their skin, engaged them in French conversation, and, when they tired of splashing in the water, fished for them *à la palangrotte*, five hooks on a line, with bits of bread as bait, lowered from a rock at the end of the beach so that the hooks hovered just above the sandy bottom, where tiny fish darted back and forth in the shade cast by the rock. During the twins' nap, if there were no guests in the house, the cook watched the girls, and Ben and Rachel swam. At last, wafted by the Mediterranean swell, he was no longer a virgin: they made love beyond the rock, where their feet could barely touch, in Rachel's room when she retired after dinner, in Ben's bed when she awoke in the night and abruptly wanted him.

As it happened, Rachel was rarely without guests. The exchange rate had put wind into many people's sails. Some of the great men at the helm of little magazines then beginning to bud in Rome and Paris came to Hyères in wheezing black Citroëns; others got off the train at Toulon, where Ben would meet them. They smoked Gitanes made with yellow paper, drank *pastis* in the sun and scotch when it set, and organized raucous games of *boules* under the dusty plane trees. They were friends of the writers Ben was beginning to read; later in the summer they would stay with those writers. The house filled with the boom of voices. When Ben joined in the conversations, he thought these well-pitched and resonant organs pushed his voice aside, as though it were a *deux chevaux* in the way of one of their automobiles. His accent had an overlay of strangeness of which he was always aware; it would glide out of control until, dry mouthed, he listened to his own words with panic, waiting for their end. The twins' uncle, a Mainline Philadelphia doctor, sailed over on a chartered boat that Ben learned to call a ketch. He wore lime-green shorts and a faded blue shirt. The aunt's face was covered with red blotches. They talked to Rachel about money and cruising: a world of summers he had never known, and, it seemed to him, he would never fully understand, yawned before Ben. He was late and would never catch up; their awkward careless grace was destined to elude him; his pleasures, his happiness, lay only between Rachel's legs.

I have dwelt on this interlude because Ben himself returned to it so often in our conversations: he said it was the summer that determined the direction his life took thereafter. When

I questioned Rachel recently, in the course of writing this story, she agreed with Ben's view; in fact, she supplied corroborating details I had forgotten or Ben had not mentioned.

At the end of that season of miracles, he returned to the States on the now-familiar student ship. As he made his way home, seasickness combined with bitter reflections to dissipate his sense of displacement and defeat. After all, was he not, although perhaps the youngest and least well prepared, at the head of his college class, and had not he won his place effortlessly, without care or plan, while the struggles of those happier classmates, rich with memories of golden summers, purchased mediocrity? Did not his thoughts outrun what the others trumpeted so confidently around Rachel's table? And was it not he, once the Little Lord Fauntleroy of a Central European town with a name these Houyhnhnms could not pronounce, and now denizen of a Jersey City they smirked at, who slept with Rachel, whose cock was nightly sucked by her, who was so miraculously able to love Sarah and Rebecca and to be loved, yes loved, by them? What did it matter if all his younger years had been emptied of meaning by the New World? He would shut a gate of bronze upon them. The storehouse of all the shame and vulnerability in his life would be locked; a private museum of curios with but one visitor, himself, to stare at the degraded and rejected lares and penates. Only new acquisitions and artful forgeries would be on show. Clothes make a man and, with even greater power, so do lessons learned in the right sort of childhood. Within the limits of verisimilitude, he would have both; to his own skill he foresaw no limit. He repeated the words of a sampler Rachel owned: "Give me, O Lord, Thy early grace, nor let my soul complain that the young morning of my days has all been spent in vain."

AS IT TURNED OUT, the laying of Ben's new foundations did not seem to involve many outright lies. If one paid close attention, one might notice, sooner or later, some of his strange zones of unreliability in recollection—when had he made a crucial acquaintance, under what circumstances had he learned to jump a horse (if indeed he knew how!), how could so many experiences appropriate for a gentleman have been compressed into the few years that separated him from the prehistory of wartime Europe, or from the nameless high school in New Jersey through which he had passed briefly on his way to Harvard and a New Life? These slips surprised in a man with a memory and a bent for precision as prodigious as his. But Ben was very careful; he would correct the occasional improbable inconsistency in dates and, in the end, offer explanations that, for all the envelope of self-effacing charm, came down to his having been in these subjects, as in all others, a rapid and gifted student. One surmised that he had quietly put himself through a crash course in living the good life—good above all in its difference from the one in which he had feared he might be confined. It was a course of such rigor that the boot camp at Quantico, which seemed to have taught him exclusively map reading and how to maintain a parade-ground posture, must have felt, in all but its physical-fitness drills, like a comfortable spa.

And for all my well-bred prejudice against strivers and achievers—we said in my family that one was, one did not become, even as Boston matrons need not buy hats because they have them—I saw nothing repellent, and certainly nothing dishonoring in what he had done. It had been performed so pleasantly and effortlessly. As his ascent to gentility proceeded (I rely on Rachel's account of how the first grand friends were acquired at college), Ben neither checked at the door nor took trouble to emphasize the fact that he was a refugee Jew; probably, the worst that can be said is that he seemed to expect to be forgiven for it and did not appear vexed when he wasn't. Along the same line, Ben did not, in my opinion, make an effort either to hide or to display his Jersey City connection—more particularly, his baffled parents while they still lived. Who except those parents could blame him for not putting them at the center, as it were, of his social life? The family home in Jersey City was easy enough to reach from Park or Fifth Avenue, but where, in that dusty street of red row houses, was the tennis court or pool in which Ben's friends might disport themselves, and were those parents, starved for the presence of their strange, furtively obsessed only child, of a mind to receive those friends with the equanimity and graceful ease Ben might have wished?

I used to amuse myself—and perhaps Ben as well—by rehearsing with him scenes that would have gone with the life he was beginning to live so successfully. For instance: His truly good-looking mother and father, in their worn but easeful togs, relax after the day's toil. They are happy that Ben and his merry band of revelers stop by unannounced. In a matter-of-fact, casual way the father is offering a choice of drinks—perhaps slivovitz (nothing wrong with being true to one's ethnic habits) and martinis shaken by Ben upon paternal urging; the old man is telling dryly humorous stories of prewar courtroom triumphs, with just a hint of disparagement, drawing therefrom lessons for today's humbler activities. Meanwhile, the mother flirtatiously upbraids a young man for never coming to see her alone or—stroke of genius!—explains to an attentive Rachel when a gardenia begins to need repotting.

The reality—I knew Ben's parents and sometimes actually took the train to Jersey City without Ben's urging—was less comical. Irretrievably diminished by America, the severe, confident civil-law pleader now operated a small insurance business for a clientele of immigrant friends; his once-languid wife answered the telephone and pored over claim forms in the downstairs office. Love and pride (who else had a son like Ben, if only he would be reasonable?), confusion about the road that brilliant son had taken, and dread of the road ahead of them—thin days dragging on in that decaying place until some final bad end—no, these were not themes Ben cared to have developed for the general public. A friend such as I sufficed.

The mother had the good luck to die first. In the two years of his ultimate loneliness, the father's principal distraction was Ben's divorce: a chance for the old courtroom fox to guide and restrain his impetuous banker son. One might have thought the whole thing would be simple enough. Rachel and Ben had had no children together, and, what with her own and her first husband's money, Rachel did not think it really worthwhile to press a man with no capital for alimony. But an unexpected element envenomed the proceedings. It turned out that while Ben was willing to be convinced that Rachel was through with him, in his opinion that fact was an insufficient reason for severing his ties with Sarah and Rebecca. He held that these raven-haired matching adolescents were his daughters in fact, if not in law. Did not Rachel know that he would not, he could not have others? This deficiency had been, after all, at the time when it mattered, one of his prime qualities: explosion upon explosion within her, torrents of effluvia mixing, and no fear of conception! Now he wanted wages for the hours he alone had spent on their care—changing diapers, pulling on snowsuits, sliding down icy hills, pacing past dinosaur displays, reading aloud—greater in number than Rachel's and all the nurses', mother's helpers', and babysitters' hours combined. And he had conquered and kept their love; of this he was sure. His lawyer would prove it; justice had to prevail. Ben's father listened. He heard the twins. He claimed a world record for listening to Rachel. In the end, there was no trial, but there was (as Ben's Wall Street lawyer put it) a deal: so long as the twins wished, they would spend part of their vacations with Ben, there would be dinners with him, and, if schoolwork allowed, perhaps occasional weekends. In this way Ben came to think that, however high the waves might billow around him, the precious cargo would be saved: Sarah's and Rebecca's childhoods, the delicate, miraculous realization of his dreams.

Like most such arrangements, the deal did not hold for long. Rachel returned to Boston or, more precisely, to the family acres on the North Shore. Sarah became a boarder at Milton, and, over Ben's tactless and quaint objection that she did not need instruction in breaking farm machinery, Rebecca went far north in Vermont to progressive Putney. Tucked into unoccupied corners of midterm vacation, the dinners took place mostly in the familiar pomp of the Boston Ritz, the twins tasting Chambertin under the indulgent eye of the headwaiter, who was Ben's friend. That hamburgers could have been eaten somewhere, without the benefit of crystal chandeliers, and shared with classmates clad in jeans did not occur to Ben. To meet Ben the twins wore the kilts and cashmeres he packed from London; in the lobes of their ears (pierced, he would claim, when his back was turned) glowed his peace offering—pink-hued pearls lovingly chosen in Tokyo.

During the second Christmas vacation, Sarah stood him up without warning: friends were staying with her. She laughed queerly at his telephoned suggestion that she might have brought them. Ben returned to the table and a closed-faced Rebecca. It was too bad her genius sister Sarah hadn't shown up, she informed him; she knew Ben thought everything about her own friends and Putney was dumb, but it took someone really dumb like her to want to hang around the Ritz; he should know his Wallace Stevens freaked her out. Heading for Beverly Farms on Route 128, driving her back to her mother's home very slowly, Ben told her a story: In the king's palace, the carpet of childhood is woven by a blind weaver with silk and wool of many colors from many spools. His fingers have learned the outlines of figures he must give shape to, but not the placement of the colors; his master changes them each year. When the child is grown, the master and the prince or princess who was that child examine the

work and the weaver is lashed with whips or praised and
released from toil for a while, according to their pleasure.
He, Ben, is that weaver. Rebecca remained silent. When Ben
turned to look at her, he saw that she was asleep.

The next summer, like a murderer returning to the scene
of the crime, Ben rented a house on an island off Hyères
for his month of vacation. There was a terrace crowded by
bougainvilleas, a beach below, and a fisherman's boat with a
two-stroke motor that took all of Ben's strength to start. An
Italian woman cooked. Sarah and Rebecca turned the color
of copper in the sun. The tops of their bikinis off, bandannas
in their hair, toes of arched feet touching, they lay foot to
foot on the stone balustrade like rococo Indians.

Ben's heart ached with happiness and gratitude. He had
not asked any of his friends to stay with them—there were
people he knew on Porquerolles he could invite occasionally
to dinner; L'Arche de Noé served bouillabaisse and the best
profiteroles in the world when they got tired of pasta; Saint-
Tropez was but two hours away. Mostly, however, the twins
and he would fish *à la palangrotte*, as before, and dive for sea
urchins. They would read the piles of books he had brought;
the record player in the staid mahogany cabinet seemed to
work, they would listen to music. The telephone also was
working. From Antibes, where she was staying at Eden Roc,
Rachel called each evening to talk to the twins. She was
lonely; the hotel was expensive; one could water-ski in Antibes; boys from Andover, whose parents she knew, had a
catamaran. By the end of the week, Sarah and Rebecca had
gone to visit their mother; Ben had arranged to have them

driven over. When the same driver went to fetch them, the young ladies were out sailing. A day or so later, Rachel called to say the twins would stay with her: she had already reequipped them with bikinis and beach towels; he could bring the rest of their stuff to New York when he returned and mail it from there; he should be grateful he was on Porquerolles and did not have to pay Antibes prices.

I knew you could not be trusted, she added, I was right to be next door. How did you dare to fix it so you would be alone there with those beautiful girls, staring at their breasts! This was not the first time that Rachel had accused Ben of deviate conduct or desires. As he reviewed her words, however, first in rage and then coldly, with great care, he came to think that some of Rachel's inspiration must have come from the twins: it was possible that this was what they thought. In such case, he would henceforth keep his distance. He was truly alone.

AS BEN'S EXECUTOR and devisee of all his papers (as well as of his collection of neckties, cuff links, and shirt studs), I retrieved, with the help of Ben's distraught secretaries, file folders of papers from his offices in New York and Paris and, from warehouses, serially numbered, sealed cartons. Each bore a label with the words "Pandora's Box" written on it in Ben's hand. There were also documents and tapes of his dictation in the hotel in Geneva.

Thus I came into possession of Ben's pocket notebooks and diaries with notations (often illegible) of the events of the day that lay outside his business life—what he had eaten at each meal and in whose company—dates on which the reading of a book was commenced or finished, streets down which he had walked in foreign cities, as well as numbers, algebraic symbols, and little drawings to which I never found a key. On certain blank pages of these diaries—but also on sheets of paper clipped together or rolled and held by rubber bands—were lists of women's names: sometimes the full name was given and sometimes only the first name and an initial in lieu of the surname. Occasionally, one or two letters appeared on a line, without a name. Were these initials? Some names were followed by dates. Having known Ben and at least the New York world he had moved in so very well, I realized that these were records of his more ephemeral "possessions," and gradually I came to deduce that they had been made in airport departure lounges, on trains, or while Ben pretended to listen to financial presentations. He wrote them to test his memory or to break in a new fountain pen or perhaps for insertion in the curriculum vitae he would present to the arbiter of some ultimate place of repose— much as another man might have cataloged articles he had published in learned journals. The lacunae in certain of the lists and the inconsistencies, which at first I found surprising, I came to relate, in moments of frustration, to what in the past I had sometimes assumed to be Ben's mythmaking. At other times, I adhered to another, more benign explanation: Could it not be that Ben was capable of forgetting, that his memories became confused, and that, at least once in a while, his attention flagged?

Much later, when I was brought to reflect bitterly on what

must have been a signal Ben had tried to give—speaking to me so insistently and mysteriously of a novel by Pierre Jean Jouve—a signal that I had not understood but that could have been a plea for help, I read, as though in contrition, much of that writer's work and came upon the following passage, which I have translated:

> A notebook is found, containing all these names of women, with and without addresses, a chaos of names: sluts, you say, and "useful addresses." But that entire notebook, if only because it is so jam-packed, cannot correspond to experience. A man responsible for a great task could not have entered so many women. That entire notebook contains figures which correspond to one Figure only, before which the Poet is a Supplicant. It is a vow of union to the woman who belongs to all, and to all women, and thereby the notebook dissolves into a prayer. All these names adored under the vestment of nudity intercede for the poet.

I have wondered whether there too was a sign Ben had intended me to decipher.

But the most precious content of the lode of trivia, mischief, and lyric self-expression Ben bequeathed to me were notes, many typed (when Ben was traveling with his portable Olivetti), others written in his large slanting hand, rarely dated, a large majority filed in apparent chronological order under the name "Notaben"—the sort of pun of which Ben was monotonously fond—and a few letters addressed to him. Ben did not make copies of letters he had written, but there were in Pandora's Boxes some drafts of letters he had written in

French. Apparently, he was not sure of getting them right on the first try.

Some of these materials are reproduced in the narrative that follows. I changed certain names and details that might reveal the identity of my cousin, the woman I call Véronique.

II

TOWARD THE END of August 1969, Ben moved to Paris, taking charge of his bank's long-established office in the place Vendôme. At the time, for a young partner, this was the equivalent of canonization. For someone of his tastes, it could also be seen as the entry into the Garden of Earthly Delights: when Ben turned his back on the green and gold expanse of his Empire desk top, his eye would behold the verdigris of Napoleon's column; he would lunch at the Ritz unless, to please a client sophisticated enough to know that Maxim's must be shunned in the evening, he determined to stroll down the rue Saint-Honoré to the rue Royale and welcome his lunch guest in the sanctum of the omnibus. It was understood that the assignment was for the usual period of two or three years only, and that he would continue to follow matters of certain clients occasionally requiring his presence in New York. Ben decided to keep his apartment on Central Park West: it was where Sarah and Rebecca had last stayed with him. Now that they were in college they might be induced to return—especially if he wasn't there! The day before he sailed we took our customary noontime meal. Although we were in Vermont as we were every August, I came down to the city for the occasion. He handed me a set of keys and said the maid had been told to expect my presence on weekdays: for work, he emphasized, not trysts, it being Ben's theory that I used my cubicle at the magazine principally as a telephone booth and would never finish the book I was writing on Indian use of the land in Maine unless I was removed to the comfort and silence of his library. Another gesture of affection was to come: Ben remembered that my wife and I had not been to Europe since our honeymoon. Would we not leave the children in the care of the current señorita and visit him in Paris as soon as he had a place to live? He was going to look for one that would make good memories for him and for us. I accepted on the spot. Prudence would agree—of that I was sure. Like many of Ben's friends' wives, she had a soft spot for him.

Here, I later learned, is how Ben found his Paris apartment.

Excerpt from Notaben 73 (undated):

What is a nightmare? A daydream come true. So holds an old Bessarabian proverb I will use as the epigraph of my treatise on apartment hunting, but only if it translates well into many languages. My work will be a worldwide success.

The little marquis *de rien du tout* took me to see one at the very top of Montmartre. Climb lots of stairs, unacceptable mental image of me and my bags—assuming Figaro doesn't rush down to get them. Effort rewarded by heart-stopping views: (1) All of Paris, stretching beyond the Invalides. In the slight mist, as I squint against the setting sun, it lies before me like a burnt offering. (2) The owner's long legs, tanned and creamy, only a little soft in the thigh (she must be over 40). Am I reaching an age where a woman a couple of years older than I will begin to seem too old?

I love the century I live in. She receives her prospective tenant in a miniskirt that stops at the crotch; she is a sun worshiper, she explains, as she leads us up a spiral-ladder contraption to the terrace on the rooftop (an even better view of the legs with a hint of the twin gates between). I forbear from confessing I am a blind leg worshiper—must touch, must feel, must enter the temple (on my knees if need be). She tells me she will principally worship in her native Venezuela for the 3 years to come, but has a little house in Bora Bora for intensive retreats. Perhaps I would care to come.... The word is like a bell; I switch to the language of Descartes to recover my composure. Mind made up this lodging will not do but *commerce oblige*. We admire the terrace, study the watering system for the hibiscus, descend the ladder (no view), penetrate the mistress bedroom done in gray leather, possibly to set off the collection of omnipresent native masks, hats, and clubs (just like dildos only bigger), two guest rooms (smaller dildos, perfect for Jack and dear Prudence), etc.

At last I sense I have been polite long enough.

If only you were not leaving, *chère* Madame, if I could be your grateful lodger, it would be a cinch: your humble servant would pant to pay FF15,000/ month plus charges, plus whatever it takes in cash

under the table for Juanita/Susanna, merely for the
privilege of being near you, huddling in the smallest
room with the smallest dildos, pardon, clubs, but
as it is . . .

And so I flee, and so let the marquis, his spirits
dampened, tongue loose, drive me as far as the
Opéra, where I catch a cab.

All this is nonsense, the right stuff for lunch with
Jack. Nothing to do with poor Ben, mad Ben, not the
way he is now.

We are not very well, is that not so? We do not
like bumping against curbs when we drive our little
auto, even without a drop having taken, do we? And
what have you eaten, Lord Randall my son, to feel so
ill and frightened while the little marquis heads for
the Automobile Club, the two hours he wasted with
you already receding in his mind? Darkness and
loneliness, Mother. I fain would be happy but do not
know how. Meanwhile, Montmartre and the 360°
view are not for me. I will not drive my Peugeot up
those winding streets. I will not buy *boudins blancs* at
the corner charcuterie or consume them alone in that
Latin whore's nest or correct there the offering
prospectus for Biscuits Cul after my solitary meal.

Cab stuck on the way to the Left Bank. Monstrous
traffic jam at the Carrousel. Hangover returns, with it
poison gas and stomach cramps. Jack and Prudence
are *ante portes*—just like Prudence to write they are
coming before good old Ben has built his dream
house.

Mercifully, the rue du Cherche-Midi is one way the right way. Pull up at familiar building opposite rue Férou at six sharp. A few doors up the street, refurbished hotel, now full of black diplomats. No questions asked, sparkling clean chintz rooms, hard beds I've tried to death with Josiane, Christiane, Liliane (not picked for euphony, cross my heart!). Hotel's proximity of dubious value if I take the place but, with my life's twists and turns, who is to say?

Manservant opens door. Previously concealed or new since last visit. Italian—very polite. Mme de la Chapelle, née Morgan, will see me; never know whether to kiss these Franco-American hands. In her case, to be consistent, I do. Usual synoptic review of: all her Morgan and Roosevelt connections putatively alive, whether or not known to me; Rachel and what are the names of those darling twin girls; my partners over sixty—here manservant pours a martini, may the Almighty pour blessings on him; the iniquity of French taxes in all their manifestations now that the regretted Léandre de la C. is no longer here to "cope." She's getting to the point; that is why she has decided to lease but not yet sell this 18th c. pavilion, entrance from the courtyard of a banal building, on the other side its own garden, with all her furniture (reasonably good), paintings (of the period and inoffensive), bed linen, table linen, and forks and knives, and there is nothing like these toothy Long Island transplants when it comes to fixing and fitting out a house. With Léandre's sister, it would have been all show: Aubusson in the hall, *l'entre-deux-guerres* in the kitchen. With my lovely Olivia we have the Aubusson all right, but the kitchen is one where dear Ben will not mind tossing a salad, particularly if Gianni has laid it all out, as he always does, before taking his Thursday and Sunday evening. Gianni pours another martini: good man, already trying to ingratiate himself.

Jack and Prudence are in luck. Now we are in the American mode; I shake Olivia's hand on the deal. She had worried I would want to move her stuff out and move my own in. I make her happy—my clothes are all I am bringing. She thinks it charming I left my pad in NY intact. Of course, such a good building! She means that's how people used to live.

Lest she think some more and decide I am a spendthrift and so double the rent (thus far moderate), I say I will need my NY apartment for business trips; hotels now awfully expensive and unreliable. This she understands. What would she think if I said to her—so practical, so brave in her old age, willing to leave her home of 35 (or is it more?) years and move back to NY (to be sure, she too has kept her house there) just to save on taxes for her loutish lawyer son—that I couldn't bear to close the only home I have? Acquired post-Rachel! Worse, that I can't decide to transport my ten sticks of worldly goods to Paris, install those same ten sticks in some place I have first caused to be painted, decorated, etc.; that I have no idea why I do anything I actually manage to do, except, of course, my work.

That must be the point of the epigraph. I have no place I need to be (except my office) and no person I need to be with (except the boys at the office).

Admirable condition of freedom: one would suppose I might continue living at the Ritz—possibly talk the bank into paying for it—and wait to see what happens. Or, for instance, live up on Montmartre where "people" don't live. I could meet some nonpeople, spend my next vacations at Club Med. Unfortunately, I can't bear freedom. Antidote for freedom: multiply Ben's obligations. Thus, I am still one foot in New York but already I have Jack and Prudence as houseguests in Paris at a house I haven't yet looked for; thus, I must quickly find a "home" where they can be guests (a place that makes good memories, that being the idiotic phrase I had the bad taste to make); thus, with my equally renowned efficiency I find such a place and obtain possession thereof—including *il bravo Gianni*, very authentic and beautifully restored boiseries, and a parking space for my car in my very own courtyard. Car = freedom. Should I give up the parking space and the car, or console myself by the thought that I am subject to another servitude? The beastly thing will need to be serviced and either I will have to see to it or, better yet, con Gianni into taking it on!

A dream come true, right?

I am not convinced that this particular message from the other world is fully reliable. In life, Ben was not impenetrable; I presume to believe that the prospect of our visit was, in fact, welcome. This is one of the undated Notabens: When did he write it? Before our visit, as the text indicates, or later, as an exercise in style or to explain subsequent events or disappointments? The number he gave it is of little help in this respect: I have come to think that Ben numbered notes and letters at random or in accordance with a system known only to him. Most important to me, I cannot dismiss the possibility that, whenever the text was written, he was striking a pose, as he did in so many circumstances, not because he was a poseur but out of discouragement. Ben liked to joke that he was his own invention and therefore never could be certain how he really felt about anything or anybody. I wonder whether he did not sometimes try to solve the problem, and put an end to tormenting doubts, by also inventing various experimental versions of his feelings.

PRUDENCE AND I arrived at Ben's in the second half of October; we were to spend three weeks and still get back in plenty of time to make ready for Thanksgiving and Christmas. We both have large families, Prudence's only slightly smaller than mine. She promised not to do all her shopping in Paris. Fortunately, Ben had warned us that the days when one could find charming little bargains for all the aunts and nieces were over. Bloomingdale's had the same merchandise at half the price.

We were as happy as clams in the house on the rue du Cherche-Midi. Although the weather was still mild, so that in late morning and early afternoon we could open the French windows leading from the drawing room to the little walled garden, the leaves of the acacia trees had turned yellow and red and dotted the ground cover of moss and creeping ivy; sometimes they stuck to the white, grinning face of the marble goddess (Ben claimed it was Pomona) he arranged to have installed in the center of the garden—to keep us company— the day after our arrival. He was right; this absence from the children, from the magazine, from my unwritten book, and Prudence's dance class was a cure that had come just in time. Ben left for the office before we rose; a silent and grave Gianni ministered to our breakfast needs, made up our room, and whisked away my shirts while we drank coffee and read the *Tribune*, awaited instructions about lunch, lit fires at the first hint of a chill when the day waned. I think it amused Ben to learn that Olivia de la Chapelle and I were distantly related—through the Alsops—and that my grandmother and she had in fact been friends as girls; he enjoyed the savor of New York connections. In consequence, he had introduced me to Gianni as the countess's nephew, a quality that may have accounted for Gianni's benevolent patience about our mealtime habits. Prudence had discovered Fauchon: whatever might have been agreed about lunch, she would arrive with her packages of pâtés, goat cheese, and marinated mush-rooms that simply must be put on the table, fruit-flavored teas and tea cakes to be added to the afternoon repertory of refreshments, and new jams for breakfast. I managed to have lunch with Ben only once, in part to visit his office but principally to discuss the trip the three of us were planning to take, as a sort of extended weekend, to the châteaux of the Loire. He made it clear that in Paris lunch was even more a part of the working day than in New York; we would instead see each other in the evening, whenever possible.

I knew some people in Paris, American journalists and writers, and would have liked to introduce Ben around—he did not appear to move in that circle. Interesting friends he used to see with Rachel had gone back to the States or lived in the French countryside, and I suppose he was reluctant to look up, on his own initiative, people who might be said to belong to her. I got the feeling that he spent his free time (of which there seemed to be little) among a collection of rather tattered French types, some with sonorous names, and all connected, when you came right down to it, with a man called Guy Renard, a fashion photographer very aware of his own charm, whom Ben had met in Porquerolles. Most of them, perhaps all, came to the house to drink champagne at the beginning of our first week. Since these people seemed impervious to Prudence's and my French, and themselves ran out of English conversation at the end of two sentences, my conclusion that they were a bum lot did not rest on much; perhaps it was not really necessary to remove Ben from their influence. But that is what I nevertheless concluded. I was pursuing this goal when I hinted to him at lunch, after we settled our travel plans, that I might get together a group of writers for drinks at the rue du Cherche-Midi or, if he found it more convenient, at the bar of the Ritz. Ben said quickly that I should by all means give a party, that it must be at his place (Gianni would do it all or get help), and that he would probably join us—it all depended on the hour the guests came and left and where he stood with some negotiations that required evening telephone calls to New York.

I understood at once it was unlikely that he would come to meet my friends in his own drawing room, even though they included the Paris-based *New York Times* political reporter he most admired. A flush of annoyance passed over me; there was an unpleasant mixture of boorishness, pride, and envy under the surface of Ben's carefully polite reaction to my proposal, which set my teeth on edge. I was at the point of telling him that for his own sake he should cut it out but stopped myself—for how was this bit of self-improving ablation to be performed?

To anticipate events, I was, of course, right about the party: Ben first called to say he was delayed; our friends in due course suggested we all go out to dinner; his secretary rang to say we must not wait, he would try to catch up with us at the restaurant. We stayed late, not exactly waiting for Ben but drinking too much new wine; he never came. When we got home that night—Ben was still out—I said to Prudence that perhaps he had acted wisely. He might not have wanted to risk being put forward by me as his interesting banker host only to find that the guests, after volubly admiring his establishment, drinking his liquor, and eating his foie gras canapés, had departed with no likely sequel to his hospitality.

For the moment, though, having decided not to launch an attack across the lunch table, I said I was grateful for his generosity and asked if his life was indeed as celibate as it seemed. Or was he being discreet out of respect for Prudence?

Ben laughed—he had seen how put out I was. Having carefully cut and lit a cigar, he said, No, I don't practice celibacy, I practice sexual hygiene—rigorously! Do you want to hear about it?

I nodded my head. A set piece, as though an actor playing the part of Ben had stepped toward the footlights, followed.

My sessions with Dolores are at lunchtime, he intoned, on Mondays and Fridays and usually at teatime on Wednesdays, subject to holidays, the will of God and my clients, and, most particularly, the reliability of the lady's husband—in principle, he doesn't lunch at home. Never on weekends, that's when he is around and does eat lunch. She comes to my house, but it seemed awkward to keep to our routine and not upset yours; besides, Dolores's pad is nice—just under the roof of the Palais Royal. It's a shame not to use it. Off her bedroom she has a little balcony with geraniums, sunlight always on the verge of flooding it. We might well do our exercises there regularly, but Gianni serves just the sort of light *cocotte*'s meal I approve of, and his point of view doesn't matter—in fact it is altogether benign—whereas Dolores's maid is devoted to the husband and has to be got out of the way, which is a nuisance. But you don't really want me to go on about how I keep in form, or do you?

I assured Ben of the intensity of my interest and, more precisely, my curiosity.

He said, Now you have asked for it, I don't have an appointment until after three, I will tell as much as modesty permits. There isn't just Dolores. Don't forget Paris has been my port of call for a long time, but let's start with Dolores— I actually call her Do, because she will do anything and I can't bear her name. Can you remember my dentist in New York? I once gave you his name, when Rachel and I were still together. He was our family dentist, and I told you that Rachel claimed he would rub his erection against her arm while he was drilling. Well, he never did that to me, and he was actually my first guest in Paris, though not at rue du Cherche-Midi—he stayed in the spare bedroom of my suite at the Ritz. Before I sailed, I went to have my teeth cleaned. As usual, when his assistant had finished, he came in to tug at my tongue, and like an idiot—except that God looks after idiots—I told him I was moving to Paris. I had not even opened wide or bitten down or what have you, and already he was asking if he could spend a few days with me; he just happened to be going to Paris, too, though fortunately not on the same boat. The few days turned into a week. That was all right; I wasn't around much and neither was he.

Anyway, the first Sunday morning after I moved into my present digs the telephone rings. Barely awake (pun intended) I answer; a female voice speaking Iberian French wants to speak to the doctor. I explain ever so politely that he left Paris while I was still living in a hotel. Oh, she says, you must be that *très gentil Monsieur Ben*; I say, At your service; and, believe it or not, the voice expresses a keen desire to come at once to see me. I plead for two hours' delay; it is granted. At the appointed minute, the doorbell rings— Gianni being off, I open the door. Henna-red hair, raincoat, white poodle. Ever affable, I ask the lady and the dog to come in. When Dolores, hand kissed, poodle let loose, allows me to take her coat I see she is wearing black shiny leather from neck to boot tops: a sort of birthday suit, because my keen eye detects no bump or line bespeaking such nonessentials as underpants or bra. I offer champagne; she accepts; we sit down on the *causeuse* and begin to chat. Here is the story: Dr. Banks the dentist filled her and her husband's teeth in New York and by and by was filling her other cavities as well. The husband is in the shipping business—why that called for his moving from New York to Paris I haven't found out—here she mainly studies yoga. That the old drill wizard wanted to resume his ministrations between visits to the Louvre is not surprising, but imagine my astonishment when she told me he recommended me to her, saying I would begin where he left off. Of course, he was right to count on me and I have been very grateful—I have even sent him a case of wine. I call my activities with Do hygiene, in part because of the association with oral hygiene but mostly because it's all so neatly executed and repetitious: regular position, followed by top-to-toe, followed by her on me, and then, once a week, on Wednesdays, unsolicited she opens her back door to me. Why on Wednesdays—it's a good question, but you know me, I only ask questions at work or when I am trying to find my way to the post office, so I really don't know. If you think there is a strange, faint odor in my bedroom I will tell you its reason. Do's poodle is always around to watch us and the beast is incontinent!

I told Ben I felt he should round out, if that was the right expression, our tour of Paris by letting Prudence and me meet the lady, but he categorically refused.

It would be like having you to lunch with the squash pro,

an excess of zeal. Besides, if you want a tour of Ben by Night, it would have to be more extensive, and it's subject to changes and cancellations without previous notice and without refund. Right now there is also a bookstore owner with radical political views, flat chest, and capacity for instant orgasm; a cousin of Guy's who smells of Gitanes, swears, and has one gold front tooth; and an oversexed Cockney bank employee—I assure you not of my bank!—who loves to eat and has such awful table manners that when I take her out to dinner I wish I could hide behind a newspaper just not to see what she is doing with her fingers. All of this is good hygiene and moderately good fun, even though the loss of my "precious bodily juices" is huge. I just don't want to mix my gymnastics with you and Prudence and what one might call my more permanent life.

Those were days when Dr. Strangelove and General Jack D. Ripper never failed to amuse us; I rose from the table in the best mood. Ben had told me that rue du Cherche-Midi was a street of monasteries and convents. I was happy to be able to think that Ben did not, after all, return from work to the la Chapelle elegance only to live there like a monk. On Saturday morning, as arranged, we left for the Loire.

Notaben (undated and unnumbered):

Yesterday, I took the Cockney to a party given by her friend Marianne. It seemed wise to skip the fiesta Jack and Prudence were organizing at rue du C-M for the fashion and Vietnam War gurus of the *Trib*. I know the type without having the honor of knowing

the individuals—stick French words indiscriminately
into their English, accent like breaking stones, voices
loud (competitive decibel production), breath sour
(effect of whiskey? cigarettes? too much shouting?),
passion for undiscovered bistros known only to other
Americans.

Marianne lives *au diable*—obscure cold street,
wrong side of the Champ de Mars. Two maids'
rooms (partition knocked down) in one of those
bourgeois buildings that teach revolution to servants
and justify their body odor. Elevator for the masters;
brutally steep, metal stairs for the servants lead to the
seventh floor, where are all the *chambres de bonnes*.
No individual WCs; one Turkish toilet for the whole
floor, crosshatched outlined feet where you place your
feet and squat and strain. In the middle of the
corridor on which these rooms (cubicles?) give, a
cold-water faucet. That's all. Marianne has a hose she
attaches to it, which leads to her room. There it can
be in turn connected to a bottled-gas heater. From the
heater another hose leads to the ceiling and ends in a
shower head. A curtain encircles the entire
installation. On the floor, directly under the shower,
is a tub to collect the water from Marianne's
ablutions. Reason for my mastery of these details:
before the last guests (including Cockney and me)
leave, Marianne demonstrates its use and, extensively,
her own charms. Someday must ask why she shaves
all her body hair except under the arms. Based on
investigations to date, this is not the fashion here.

But I am getting ahead of my story—if there is
one to be told.

Marianne's room dimly lit—that is the fashion—
and filled with French and English receptionists and
"hostesses"; the latter are young women who show
one around "salons," i.e. exhibitions of anything one
might think of—books, washing machines, crockery
from Limoges, cheeses of France. . . . Two plaster
copies of 18th c. heads, one real Louis XVI chair. No
American girls; they don't fit in; too ambitious?
Aggressive?

Sociological note. Solid French-Catholic families
don't believe in education for their nubile and
lascivious daughters. Once these adorable young
things with first-class manners and unfurnished heads
leave the convent school, they crowd into precisely
such futile and underpaid occupations; they are so
pleased to find a job and "studio" (meaning this sort
of hovel) to live in. So established, they have infinite
leisure, the Lord be praised, for lubricity!

Marianne assembled an almost equal number
of male predators. Among them, young American
lawyer with big ears that stick out like mine—works
for a firm I give some business to. Also, Gilbert de
Caille, always on the prowl, like a cat. Strange,
considering his name. We are enveloped in the odor
of sausage, Camembert, and red wine, deafened by a
French Chuck Berry. Apropos of sticking out, nothing
here sticks out more than my presence. I am older

(though Do tells me I look too young for her to be seen with), I am *un monsieur important,* I am too well dressed, I am—they think!—rich. The young lawyer, I can tell, is torn: Should he keep on fondling the blond girl's knee or talk to me—one never knows, what if I became "his" client?

The Cockney disappears. *Pipi* room? Into the stairway, to be felt up by an enterprising guest? Or can't I see her through the cigarette smoke? Gilbert approaches, puts his arm through mine. Acrid smell fills my delicate nose. He knows the Cockney. Says her *con* is in a state of constant (no pun intended by me) itch. Were he to telephone her from a café and say, Hike up your skirt, take off your underpants, and don't move, I'll be right over, she would do as he told and wait as long as it took, getting wetter and wetter.

Gilbert is surely right; no doubt speaks from experience. I leave him, go over to talk to Marianne, member now fully aroused. Like the *libraire,* she has no breasts, but vast like Venus in the hips. Asks me why I go to Amsterdam all the time. I begin to tell her—shouldn't a legal secretary be curious about Dutch holding companies and money that grows in the shade? By way of a strange non sequitur, perhaps because the vanity of all my pursuits suddenly chills me ("a man may sit at meat and feel the chill in his groin"), I change the subject. Speak to her confidingly about Rachel and the twins, and how a man who has lost his arm will sometimes feel twinges of pain where his fingers had once been. She cannot hear me over the music; goes off to pass more runny cheese.

Hours later, when we have finished our business in bed, the Cockney tells me how Marianne said I am the most sinister man in the world. My Dracula qualities not being usually manifest, knowing that they "converse" in French, I ask how Marianne phrased this in her native tongue. *L'homme le plus sinistre du monde* is the giggled reply. That's all right, lovey, say I comfortingly, she only means I am the *dreariest* of men.

We were lucky. During the entire five days we were on the road the weather remained perfect, the sky of a gentle blue, the sort one often sees in Impressionist paintings but never in America, where the light is so much harsher. It was warmer than when we had arrived; Prudence said how like an Indian summer, and Ben told her the French-Christian expression for that strange season, which is so like the gift of a pagan god. We wanted to see all that we possibly could— Prudence had studied the green Michelin and pored over the detail maps—we hoped Ben wouldn't want to sacrifice tourism to country inns with stars before their names. As it turned out, he had a low opinion of all restaurants between Orléans and Tours and did not object to picnics, provided they could be held in a meadow on the side of a hill, preferably above a vineyard, with a flat stone or two at hand to put the food upon. There was no lack of such meadows. Ben would shop early, to be sure we had our provisions before the shops closed for the sleepy lunch hour, composing meals of sausage, sardines, and cheese, bread to be eaten on the side, against the judgment of Prudence who would have preferred to make sandwiches; we drank local red wine—Chinon, Champigny, and Bourgueil—fragrant and, according to Ben, no more apt to turn our heads than Evian. He would drink the wine like water, he announced; after all, he wasn't the chauffeur. That was because, immediately at the start of the trip, he turned the wheel over to me, explaining that some sort of nervousness or distraction, he wasn't sure of its nature, made him drive badly, to the point where he thought he was all the time on the verge of running into things.

While we stretched on the grass in the sun, and over dinners, Prudence talked about French Renaissance architecture. She had studied art history at Radcliffe, her memory was good, and Ben seemed unable to tire of asking her questions. They were wonderful questions, so well organized to lead up the evolutionary chain from Blois to Chambord that I wondered if Ben was absorbing new information or exquisitely keeping up his end of a leisurely cultural baseline volley to let his best friend's wife show off. I didn't much care where the truth lay: Prudence was in seventh heaven. We were even less abstemious at dinner. One evening, Ben announced that while he and I would split the bill for the food as usual, the wine would be on him. We ate crayfish as a first course—the specialty of the hotel's brightly lit restaurant with little table lamps made out of gnarled vine roots—and with them drank a local wine and then, when it came to pheasant stewed with cabbage, two bottles of a Beaune–Enfant Jésus '59 of a price so prodigious that Ben suggested we pretend for the rest of the meal that we were his bank's valued clients, with taste and strength to match. He was celebrating an anniversary of sorts, he told us, a trip to Burgundy with Rachel in the year of that wine, precisely when the grapes were being brought in. They had left the twins at home. One evening in Beaune Rachel and he drank that very wine (selected, he assured us, without sacrilegious intent on his part), from the same producer, Monsieur Bouchard, but of the '47 vintage, and that was the year in which his father chose Jersey City for their family home in the New World, a coincidence that seemed to him at the time full of tragicomic meaning he now could not remember, perhaps because this '59—so far as he was concerned a better year in all respects than '47—had addled his brains. Rachel and he had finished one bottle that evening and made a good dent in the second, sending what was left to the chef with their compliments, and made their way, arms around each other's waist, to their room in the Hôtel de la Poste, so justly famous for huge, hard beds, made expressly, or so it seemed, so that those Chevaliers du Tastevin who managed to survive the twenty-kilometer automobile return trip from the banquet in Vougeot could snore in sodden bliss until the onset of morning hangover. Only Rachel and he did not snore—not right away in any case—they made love in those sheets that were like some snow country.

The chocolate soufflé came: Ben detected unsuitable lumps, consequence of haste and careless stirring, allowed Prudence to talk him out of sending it back to the kitchen, which he claimed he would have done only to prove to the chef that we paid attention to what we ate. Instead, he asked for '59 champagne to console us for life's imperfections. We drank to our next trip—we would go to Avallon, Vézelay, and Beaune next spring, if Prudence's parents would take the children during Easter vacation—and then to the twins: he wished them and associated delusions bon voyage. At the table next to us were four men who looked like garage owners. They left after much embracing of the *patron* and the *patronne*. We were now the only guests in the dining room. Whether to mark his contentment with what we had consumed or to speed us to our room, the *patron* offered us old brandy. We clinked glasses, and when I stood up I was grateful that our room was only one flight of stairs away. Ben too was tipsy, tipsy enough to say he hoped that what we had eaten and drunk at table would not detract from pleasures that should follow, and how, in his own case, he was not sure he would even manage to sacrifice to absent loves before sleep overcame him.

Excerpt from letter, dated September 1975, from Rachel to me:

I've forgotten the name of the wine in Beaune.
Isn't it like Ben to have such a thing up his sleeve,
unless he had forgotten it also and only said you
were drinking the same wine to give his story higher
color. That too would be like him. Why did this sort
of thing stick in *your* memory? Were you taking notes
on Ben even then?

Whatever its name, the wine was very good. I chose it and I paid for it. He didn't tell you that, I suppose. Or did you both take it for granted?

The rest of the evening I remember more vividly. Before I undressed, he asked to do something we had never done before, right away, in haste. He hurt me, and when I told him, he said he didn't care, it was a part of the pleasure. Later, in bed, he tried to be nice but I told him it was too late and he gave up. So while I cried he lay in my bed, although there were two beds in the room, utterly silent, stiff from self-righteousness. You couldn't hear or feel him breathe. It was always like that. Once he began to feel guilty and humiliated he couldn't even try to make things better.

Chenonceaux was the most distant château we were going to visit. When we walked down the long gallery, the river trembling green and gold under the windows on both sides, I told Ben that my great-uncle Hugh had been one of the convalescent soldiers quartered in that very room during the last months of the Great War; utterly lacking in originality, he married his nurse, a young woman of good family, and settled near her parents' place in the Perche region of France to raise horses. There was one child, a son; they sent him to Groton and then to Harvard; he, too, made his life in France, was taken prisoner by the Germans when the advance began after the *drôle de guerre*, and came home only in '45. From then until his death in '55 or '56, he was the Paris banker and mentor for all Americans with bank accounts above a certain size that were validated by the right social connections. He had a daughter, my ravishing cousin Véronique, who was educated first by the nuns in Paris, like her mother, and then at Vassar. That is why I knew her; on weekends she often stayed with my parents in New York. For a number of years now she had been married to a lawyer, handsome and polite in an intensely French manner, and related to everybody. They had an apartment at a fashionable address and a place in the country somewhere near Paris. My mother had seen it and had been favorably impressed. If Ben wished, I would bring us all together during the last week Prudence and I were to spend in the rue du Cherche-Midi—he might like my cousins better than my fellow journalists!

Looking back on the days we spent in the Loire Valley, I think that I had never felt so close to Ben or, allowing for the occasional unevenness of his manner, had found him so tender. He said he was delighted to add two more members of my real family to the imaginary family he worked so hard on constituting; if my cousin's husband was a lawyer, bankers were his prey. He would give a cocktail party and invite some international financiers for him to meet. Thus, through my intervention, Ben became a friend of Véronique and Paul Decaze.

The entertainment for my cousins took a somewhat different shape from what we had discussed. An urgent message was waiting for Ben when we returned to Paris. Clients of his from Oklahoma, normally busy making mountains of fertilizer in that location, were to visit him in Paris on their way to Morocco for meetings about a project he had had a hand in devising.

A tax accountant, a frustrated constitutional lawyer, and an investment banker lurk inside every writer. I am no exception. I was accustomed to listening hungrily to Ben when he described his deals, to asking questions I considered penetrating, and to following new developments when Ben returned from his victorious campaigns.

Thus I knew that the idea in this case was to improve an ancient but rich mine, to build a plant near its site, with supporting facilities so modern that a mere handful of expatriates at the controls of computers could operate it without the usual local sweepers and bearers, and to transform Moroccan phosphates into a product whose quality would match the Oklahoma stuff's. The market for this sort of fertilizer was scheduled to boom even as hunger was eradicated worldwide. The Oklahomans looked for huge profits to be realized in the rosy but quite certain future. Ben's firm would be paid, in cash, "up front," as he put it, time and time again: when the contracts were signed and sealed, when commercial banks recruited by it lent the hundreds of millions needed for all the works, and at least once more, when the public bought Eurobonds and whatever else might be invented to whet its appetite and repay the bank debt. Ben had been to Morocco dozens of times: not to visit the mine or the plant site, he told me, that was not his style—he claimed to hate industrial reality and boasted about never having set foot in a factory he had helped to finance—but to drink mint tea with the minister of finance, his dear friend Dr. Bensalem, and to moderate the greed of his clients and adversaries.

The Oklahomans assumed that he would accompany them to Rabat as usual. Ben decided against it. There is no absolute need for me to go to Morocco this time; I will send instead my number two, he told me. I don't want to miss your last days here, but I will invite the clients to the house and the Decazes with them. There won't be any bankers except from my office—you realize I can't let the competition romance my Oklahomans. It's far better for them to keep thinking I'm the only French-speaking American investment banker alive. Your cousin's husband may get business out of this just the same. I will also invite Guy Renard, for local color and for Véronique to have someone to talk to besides you and Prudence.

Six-thirty on Thursday was the appointed hour. Ben rushed into the house, thanked Prudence for arranging the flowers, and explained that he was just a step ahead of his guests. They had been at his office with him and his number two, brainstorming at a pace so slow that toward the end of the session Ben had found it necessary to keep jabbing his thigh with a sharp pencil to keep his eyes from closing. Then they refused to return to their hotel for a moment of rest— they called it a pit stop—so that the only reason they were not already on the doorstep was that he had told his secretary to delay the cars conveying them to the rue du Cherche-Midi. Then he ran off to his bath—a matter of principle, he said; we were to receive in his place if he was not ready.

By November, night falls abruptly in Paris. Gianni had lit the monumental lanterns above the steps leading to the house and the reflectors illuminating its lovely cream facade. On the garden side, more reflectors made Pomona gleam in the darkness. Pinecones crackled in the fireplaces at both ends of the drawing room. Either the sculptured marble mantelpieces with their inlays of black and pink had been undisturbed since the original owner had had them installed or Olivia had not spared Morgan dollars to replace them; they were splendid.

Gianni served Prudence and me champagne. It was ice-cold, as Ben required, the tulip glasses unmistakably Baccarat. Olivia and Ben would make a perfect couple, I thought, it's a pity she isn't forty years younger. Prudence put her hand to my cheek. I drew her to me very hard and held her. She had changed so little: the deadpan researcher I had met at the magazine almost fifteen years earlier and this young matron whose every secret I had explored had the same mountain of yellow hair, parted in the middle and held loosely with a ribbon at the nape, the same scrubbed clean skin, the same impatient speed in gestures. How much longer is this happiness to last, I wondered, what beast is lurking behind some door we will open late or soon? And Ben, when will he strike the tent of this particular circus, press a large check into old Gianni's palm, and, the house inventory carefully settled, broken crystal and china replaced to Olivia's beaming satisfaction, his bundles of gaiety, loneliness, and Charvet shirts loaded onto the gypsy wagon, head for some new and urgent engagement?

I did not have much time to linger on these questions. As the doorbell rang, Ben descended the stairs, blowing kisses to Prudence and waving his hand conspiratorially, encased in a blue suit exactly like the one he had worn upon arrival and should have, by all rights, just quit. It occurred to me that he had become thicker in the torso and perhaps even in the waist, a circumstance that might account for the prolifera-tion of these identical garments: Had Ben decided that this ebb and tide of contour must not stand in the way of his donning a favorite cheviot or flannel, so that there existed a lean team and a fat team? I could not tell whether Ben had merely changed his shirt and necktie or had put on just such a twin suit, possibly on the theory that an annoying difference in fit, if there was one, could be endured as the price of not letting his clients perceive that, unlike them, he had thought it necessary to change his clothes. Apart from this slight deposit left by rich sauces and wine—I had concluded they were Ben's way of confirming daily one form of his success, not an addiction—there wasn't much difference to report in his appearance that was attributable to time and not to art. Alas, he hadn't grown taller—as he liked to put it, he was a giant but only among other Central Europeans—his hair, a masterpiece of respectful barbering, was still uncompromisingly mahogany brown, the murky, Austro-Hungarian Empire features were perhaps more defined, but dominating them were those same eyes, neither quite green nor gray, with a light, like a held back tear, one used to see in the photographs of the preadolescent, pre-Harvard Ben that his mother so liked to show to visitors. I whispered into Prudence's ear, "Dressed up like a million-dollar trooper / Trying hard to look like Gary Cooper...." That song had been played at our wedding. Almost at once, I felt ashamed of the betrayal, but she smiled at me gratefully and lifted her arms. We found ourselves executing a little step and a turn.

Meanwhile, accompanied by Ben, in came the men from Oklahoma. Gianni hovered about them. I was fascinated to observe his vain efforts to separate them from their Samsonite cases and other contraptions, fashioned of black leather and similar in form to traveling cages for small pets. Mine is a bookish sort of journalism: I write about science. The rare interviews I am obliged to conduct are with people rather like the members of, let's say, the Harvard Club—fortunately more variegated now than when I joined—or the parents at my children's school. My novel was about the sort of young men the master of my house at college liked to call American orchids. In consequence, neither predilection nor experience—indeed nothing except the contemplation of fellow travelers in airport lounges—had worked to dull my reaction to Ben's clients. They were not necessarily born ugly and deformed; one supposed they had become such through parallel proclivities of body and soul. Their faces were bespectacled moons, glowing with amiability and high seriousness. Apart from one man, smaller than Ben, whose hollow chest and extreme pallor brought to mind consumption and long-neglected malaria, they carried bellies of the sort that spill over the wearer's belt in rings too thick for a double-knit suit coat to contain, even if it's belted and equipped in the back with bellows, like a shooting jacket, which was the case with many of these garments. Propped up in this manner, they distantly overhung trousers that, in turn, yearned for but never quite reached the sensible shoes below, each of which signaled the distinct painful condition of the foot inhabiting it: hammertoes, bunions, or, in the best of cases, Chaplinesque flatness. Ben introduced us to his clients, Gianni reappeared with his tray of glasses, and soon I heard Prudence laugh and cajole. The party had begun. A very polite Chicago lawyer previously concealed behind the bulk of the Oklahomans approached me, explaining he was their counsel, traveling with them the next day to Morocco. For the moment, though, both he and I were physically excluded from their group—they had surrounded Prudence.

Even grotesquely unattractive men can have a powerful effect on certain women. Prudence's voice was raised: my Manhattan geisha was discoursing on the boiseries of the *étage noble* and its remarkably well-preserved toile de Jouy. She was moving on briskly to the next subject, the wrought-iron banister—a tour of the house was bound to follow. Ben's smile was angelically benign. He had taken the short thin man by the arm and was obviously elaborating on Prudence's remarks for his sole benefit. This, too, was a new experience for me: I had never seen my friend so equably polite, and this in circumstances that I would have thought certain to spring loose his jack-in-the-box harshness and condescension. The lawyer and another man, Ben's second-in-command, who I discovered was Scott van Damm, the younger brother of a college roommate, had me pinned against the tapestry; I moved us by degrees toward the window, so that the meeting of Odysseus and Telemachus in Eumaeus's hut that it portrayed might be more conveniently explained by Prudence. During this maneuver, the lawyer continued a tale of blatant corruption of officials in Algeria, where he also did business, which shocked me—I had, like so many of my contemporaries at Harvard, thought the struggle for Algeria's liberation from the French was our own; those thin, hard-featured revolutionaries had been our heroes. Perhaps for this reason, I stopped listening to him and wondered instead about Prudence: Could she be thinking how well she was managing as the hostess she claimed Ben desperately needed? Before that reverie could become unpleasant, I heard the doorbell. The Decazes had arrived.

Writing today, I find it difficult to avoid letting an anachronistic note of irony or foreboding intrude into a description of the genial, straightforward first encounter between my cousin, her husband, and my host. Ben left the short thin man—the president of the Oklahoma company, I later learned—and greeted the Decazes before I had managed to come to their side. The talk was brisk—in fact a cross-examination of Paul conducted by Ben with hardly any preliminaries and no waste of time. As he inquired into the work Paul did, his law firm, and his experience with American businessmen, I realized that Ben had been quite serious: since I had a cousin in Paris I was fond of, he would help her husband. I supposed, in his mind, it was an elegant going-away present for Prudence and me, consistent with the tendency he had developed to regard my family as being a little on the needy side. And I could see that Ben liked Paul Decaze: he was the sort of Frenchman we then referred to as milk-fed. Born just before the war began or in its early years, brought up on a diet that made them grow to an American size, and athletic, these Frenchmen had clean teeth and a cheerful willingness to speak reasonable English. Ben said, Véronique and you must excuse us; I will throw Paul into the fish tank.

I was alone with Véronique for a moment I was hoping to prolong. She had kept the distinct sort of breathlessness I remembered from many years before, and she was even more unquestionably beautiful. I liked the way she wore her ash-blond hair in a bun that exposed to view her tightly formed, perfect ears; I admired, with a twinge of envy for Paul's or her revenues—or the way they managed them—the absolutely straight black skirt ending just at the knee, over very pale stockings, and the black knitted jacket worn over a man's shirt of dull white silk, dangerously open but revealing only a strand of pearls. Her hands ended in long, cared-for fingers. She put her arm through mine as we talked. There was nothing between Véronique and that entrancing shirt.

Mais c'est la petite Madame Decaze, comment vas-tu? I saw before us the elongated form of Ben's friend Guy Renard and, more specifically, his keen face, all profile and modeled to do justice to his name, bent over Véronique's hand where he deposited a ceremonious and satisfied kiss. Naturally, it's you, he continued in English, thus confirming the opinion I had formed of my conversational ability in his language. Where but at Ben's house, he went on, could I risk finding the only young woman in Paris who has ever resisted me, flirting with an American?

But I am practically American myself, Véronique laughed, and this man is my long-lost cousin and Ben's best friend! Paul is here too, and he really is flirting—with Ben and Ben's rich clients!

It turned out that they knew each other very well, although I like to think quite innocently, due to family ties between a certain Odile, who had been appropriately receptive to Guy's attentions, and Véronique's nearest neighbors in the village near Arpajon, where she and Paul had their country place, so that they were almost certain to see each other—on most weekends, I gathered—when the Count and Countess de Montorgueil entertained.

And it suddenly seemed utterly absurd to Guy that, having introduced Ben to all the elegant women and great houses in his acquaintance, he had never taken him to that particular château, which had no equal in the Île-de-France among properties still in private hands, and that he had never presumed to present Ben to his adorable compatriot. He took out one of those Hermès pocket diaries bound in wine-colored leather without which the French appear so lost and was ready to make concrete plans, when Ben rejoined us, saying, Monsieur Decaze is a fast worker! Before we know it he will be in Rabat, helping my friends from Oklahoma to work their way out of a French construction contract, and you will end up being very angry at me, he added for the benefit of Véronique, because while these Moroccan expeditions in themselves are profitable and perhaps even amusing, eventually they turn one's social life into a Sahara. You will never know whether you can count on your husband's being in Paris.

Guy and Ben now kissed each other. I could not help noting how quickly expressions of joyous surprise at finding Véronique at Ben's and of resolve to have Ben become a regular visitor in the countryside surrounding Arpajon and its noble dwellings entered Guy's permanent repertory. Kissing men on both cheeks instead of shaking hands and kissing women on their hands were newly acquired habits I had already begged Ben to abjure; I found them unattractive in an American, even if he was one only by adoption. An ill-timed and unfair irritation was overcoming me; it was as though my plans had already worked too well. Fortunately, Prudence reappeared at the head of the Oklahoma contingent. We drank more champagne; Ben made a toast to phosphates and their miraculous uses; Gianni presented a succession of those truly miraculous round breads, hollowed out and re-filled with paper-thin sandwiches of smoked salmon, pro-sciutto, and Roquefort that are the underpinnings of a Parisian cocktail party. It was the first time the Oklahomans had encountered them. These are *pains surprise*, surprising breads, Véronique informed the short thin man. If you tell me what hotel you are staying at, I will have a couple of them delivered to you to take to Rabat. An airplane ride won't hurt them at all!

Scott van Damm had reserved a large table at Chez José-phine, just down the street. The hour for the clients' early dinner had come—they were suffering from jet lag, upset stomachs and other perhaps even worse discomforts. Ben asked to be excused from keeping them company; the pretext, that in a few minutes he would have to return to the office to speak to New York, was one that Prudence and I had confidently expected. Quite unexpected was Paul's offer, en-thusiastically supported by Véronique, to go along to the restaurant and take Ben's place and make sure they had a true Parisian meal.

Decaze is lucky, that cousin of yours is a good business partner, remarked Ben as we returned to the drawing room. With a word or two spoken in French, he had prevented Guy from leaving with the others, and now, throwing open the

French windows that gave on the garden, and raising his arms to welcome the cold air, announced that dinner was about to be served at home: Gianni had made *gnocchi*; we would drink a great deal of good wine and then, when the mood was right, go to the bar in the rue Chauchat to hear the only real balalaika left in Paris.

III

THE FOLLOWING FEBRUARY Ben came to New York for a visit; there was a partners' meeting of his bank he wanted to attend—a matter of speaking up at the right time for Scott van Damm, who might be considered in the partnership election later in the year, or perhaps of seeing that no cracks developed in his own position in Paris. He stayed long enough for us to have lunch twice, and of course he came to dinner at home with Prudence and the children. I had recently joined a club of considerable distinction—some would say the most desirable of such institutions in the city. The thrill of leading a guest into those precincts was still fresh, and that is where I invited Ben for our farewell meal. We had already talked about my book and its slow progress. There was very little useful information about the daily life of American Indians in the precolonial and early colonial periods; almost none to reveal how they perceived their existence. I wanted a firmer grip on their truth. Ben laughed. He said (and with increasing frustration I had been coming to the same point of view) that thoughts which had not been written down could never be recaptured—except, if one has sufficient confidence, by a leap of intuition. For that, I was not ready. Ben said he knew I had not used his apartment. It was a pity, inspiration being the sister of regular working habits. In reply, I told him of Prudence's plan to take the children skiing in Idaho during Easter vacation, provided her parents made us the gift of cash they had suggested we might expect. Our next visit to Ben would have to wait until the fall.

Battle was raging in the Plain of Jars, but we did not mention Vietnam. I had come during those years to find it grating and, in the end, useless to debate the American involvement in the war with certain members of my family and close friends. Such discussions, one quickly saw, were an unpleasant waste of time; they raised questions about the values on which relationships reposed that I preferred to leave unanswered. With Ben, my disagreement was not about the conduct of the war—he had no wish to see American B-52s bomb Laos and Cambodia—or even about its merit: in fact, ever since Diem and Nhu were first fixed in our collective consciousness by the *New York Times*, he had maintained that we were backing the wrong horse in Indochina. Rather, I could not help feeling that Ben was not sufficiently American to understand a purely native aspect of the dispute about the war: the necessary, cleansing function that antiwar protest performed in the political life of the Republic. His vision of the movement—confined to pretorn blue jeans, grimy headbands, unwashed hair and feet, swaying pendulous breasts, and, indoors or out, a propensity to sit on the ground, legs outstretched, even when a chair or bench was available—usually expressed in sardonic sorties, angered me. I took it as another symptom of his irreducible Central European cultural hypocrisy: good appearance passed off for the good life, secret yearning for a brutal, punishing father translated into tolerance for the likes of Kissinger and Nixon. I wondered whether Ben's choice of service in the marines, nominally a high-spirited, aesthetic reaction against the prospect of spending, like myself and most of our friends, the two egalitarian years demanded of a peacetime draftee in the army among overweight typists and inventory clerks, had not proceeded from the same troubled source. So it seemed wiser—besides, we had only talked about me and my family—to turn the conversation to him. As usual, that meant talking in the first place about the twins.

Of Sarah, Ben said that she had done well in college. Now she was out, but instead of going for a graduate degree or getting a real job (the latter not being strictly required from a financial point of view) or having a whopping adventure— for instance, trading in coffee beans in Quito—she lived tranquilly out of wedlock with a Harvard professor of Hebrew studies at least five years Ben's senior, blessed like Abraham with children from his first wife and not in the least divorced. The wife was to blame—she refused to accept the necessary rabbinical writ from the professor. All this was taking place in Waltham, in the professor's run-down tenement, within shouting distance of Rachel's ancestral Brookline. Presumably for part-time distraction, Sarah took the morning shift at the cash register of the corner laundromat. Ben admitted that he was not above enjoying the joke on Rachel—the accusation that he was the old satyr of Porquerolles still burned in his foot like a sea-urchin spine. Less amusing to him was Sarah's view—perhaps inspired by the professor, perhaps achieved through independent analysis—

that Ben was a bad Jew, unwilling to assume his Judaic identity, and therefore unworthy of her affection.

I asked about Rebecca.

She has come to believe that I loved only her mother and Sarah, and at best tolerated her. She has no use for me, except as a high-class employment agency. All is as though I had a duty, perhaps in lieu of reparations, to get her the jobs she wants. She has her eye on some curatorial position with the Victoria and Albert in the glass department, and, believe it or not, I think I'll be able to do it! I've struck up an acquaintance with Sir Sigmund Warburg and he has been astonishingly kind about helping Rebecca. There is one small hitch: Rebecca will not come to the telephone when I call, and she doesn't answer my letters. We communicate exclusively through Rachel, which slows things down. My opinion as a banker is that I must write off Sarah and Rebecca. They are bad loans.

I am wrong to talk about this, he continued, I know my attachment to the girls has been absurdly excessive, but I find it very hard to come to terms with the obvious, fatal truth. The girls can have real or imagined complaints about Rachel—some more awful than anything I have been accused of—and Rachel will tell you and anybody else who is willing to listen that the twins are monsters. Still, in the end, something—genes? glue of family money? Rachel's being a woman?—makes their relations permanent. They have to work things out and they do. When it comes to me, after years of faithful service in the zoo, at the Museum of Natural History, and at the beach, they retired me without as much as a souvenir silver whistle. All I have left is a bad case of womb envy, baby-sitting skills, and a collection of fading snapshots I no longer keep in frames because they have become embarrassing to explain. You probably noticed that there are no photographs in my office in Paris or in the rue du Cherche-Midi. I am more divorced from the twins than from Rachel.

My own memory of him as a mother hen was vivid; we had held occasional joint picnics on the rocks above Central Park's East Meadow. Nevertheless, I didn't undertake to comfort Ben by suggesting that the twins were going through a rough period as young adults and that later their relationship would revive. I too thought that his expectations and the intensity of his feelings were excessive. Those girls were not his children; the circumstance of their natural father's being dead could not change that. And then, there were too many obstacles: Rachel's influence—she held Ben responsible for her own disappointments, and this disappointment of Ben's was a pleasant revenge; the feminist sentiments, which encouraged matrilinear groupings; Ben's hurt feelings and colossal pride. Besides, he was changing. For all his gentleness with Prudence and me—renewed evidence of which I had seen during our visit—I felt that he had, in general, become harder in manner, possibly because his self-assurance had kept pace with his success, and more set in the ways he thought befitted an elegant old bachelor. I decided to ask him instead about his sexual hygiene in Paris. The expression had stuck in my mind.

He told me there had been notable developments. Dolores's husband was moving the conjugal residence to Athens, the French tax collectors under Pompidou having become too active for his taste. Fortunately, poor Dolores had not rebelled, and Ben did not have to face the task of explaining that he was not a pillar she could lean on. The tricky problem would be to enforce the rule Ben had immediately imposed, that when she came to Paris for a visit—the husband agreed she should do that at will—she must stay at the Plaza-Athénée, like all other shipowners' wives, and not with Ben. He would receive her with joy in all his members, but only on bed-but-no-breakfast terms. Guy's cousin was opening an art gallery in Marseille and was also moving away—that didn't matter much since her services could not be compared with Do's for excitement or dependability. The Cockney was oscillating between possessiveness (she had recently asked Ben to drop her off at work after a night at the rue du Cherche-Midi; he refused, pointing out the availability of the métro at the corner of the rue de Sèvres) and tasteless, sluttish talk, possibly even behavior. For instance, it appeared that there were men among the "bosses" in her office—she had insisted on naming them—who made her "itch." New therapies, new animals for his zoo were needed, lest he be reduced to waiting for Scandinavian au pairs on the boulevard Raspail at the hour when their courses at the Alliance Française ended and they were ready for a drink with a venturesome stranger.

Viewed from my monogamous Upper East Side perspective, this last aspect of Ben's situation did not seem too depressing. But I promised to direct to him any appetizing friends who might be traveling to Paris and then asked if there weren't suitable replacements to be found among the circle of the Decazes' friends and nieces. Véronique had written to me about the favor I had done Paul by introducing them to Ben. That is how I knew that the Oklahoma clients had, in fact, retained Paul, that Paul had invited Ben to lunch, and that Ben's bank was becoming an important source of business for Paul. Ben replied that he had been glad to help Paul—especially as the work was done right. He would keep my advice in mind, but he had not yet been able to accept any of their invitations (very cordial, very tempting) in Paris or in their place in the country.

We rose from the table. His next visit would be a short one, in early April, to attend a meeting of a board of directors. We made a date for Thursday the ninth to lunch again at my club.

Notaben 273 (written on Air France stationery and dated February 1970):

On the difference between a *mujtahed* and a shithead.

A *mujtahed* is an *ulama* (Islamic scholar) recognized officially by other scholars as qualified to engage in independent reasoning on legal (therefore religious) issues. The process of such independent reasoning is *ijtihad*—one supposes the highest possible form of intellectual activity. Sometime in the XIIIth c. of our era most—perhaps all—Sunni scholars decided that the gates of *ijtihad* had been closed forever, that everything capable of being grasped by the effort of human understanding had been so perfectly set down

for the generations to follow that all that remained
was to apply precedents. That process is *taqlid*, the
opposite of *ijtihad*. Since there was no possibility—in
fact, no need for—further independent thought, no
mujtahed would again come into being.

Possibly because they are awaiting the coming of
the lost Imam and therefore must bet on the future,
Shiites have never believed in such closing of the
gates; for them, in every generation there has to be at
least one *mujtahed*, so that among them the delicious
process of *ijtihad* has continued unabated. On this
issue, the best *ulama* among the Sunni have now
rallied to the Shiite position.

This information comes from Dr. Bensalem. He
swears it is accurate, his uncle having been a great
shari'a scholar.

A shithead, on the other hand, is someone whose
head is full of shit. I have that on the authority of the
Cockney, whom I interrogated exhaustively before
giving up my initial understanding of the word. Pre-
Cockney, I understood it to denote a more superficial
condition, that of one's pate or possibly hair having
been smeared with excrement.

Why go into this? Disgust at what I have become,
fear that my head is just so packed with ignoble
desires, envy, thoughts rooted in nothing and leading
nowhere. When I traded in my chance for a life of
something like *ijtihad*, I should have picked *taqlid*.
Why not? Isn't that what they practiced so joyously

in every heder in Lithuania and Poland? Only I could have done it at a fancy law firm. As it is, I read *Business Week* instead and claim that if I am paid enough I can also interpret the *Mene, Tekel, Upharsin* on the wall.

Before Christmas, I was in Venice with the Cockney. One walks down the frozen nave of the Frari, through the arch of the choir, and suddenly perceives the Virgin ascending, her young peasant girl's feet hidden in a small, playful cloud, just out of the reach of the uplifted arms of the Apostles, who, until a moment ago, thought she was among them. Surrounding her is a crescent of cherubim, some standing or sitting on the same playful cloud, others supporting it. Above, like a flying saucer, soars the Father, propelled by two more grown-up angels; His dark-hued face is bearded and virile, resembling the vaporetto captain whose vessel I seem to board so often.

I told the Cockney I felt so "exalted and humbled" that while we were there I managed to forget about being a shithead. She paid no attention whatsoever. Perhaps she thinks I'm talking to myself. The day before, when we visited Santa Maria Formosa, I showed her the tombstone inscription near the altar that bears Hermann Wilhelm's name and mentioned that it is believed Rilke had been inspired by it. Then I launched into a discourse about Rilke's preference for Angels, lovers, animals, and trees that, as an analogy, might serve to explain my fondness for her.

Resolved: I will spend more time on sex and think less about food, clothes, and money.

Notaben 274, dated 15/3/70:

I have prepared the following notice that might, when I have had it suitably engraved, be presented by Gianni (when that invaluable man returns) on a little silver tray (naturally in a closed envelope) to all lady visitors:

> *How to Get the Most out of Monsieur Ben*
> While you are here, Monsieur will be as ardent as circumstances permit. Please respect his illusions and refrain from being more ardent than he!

Montherlant says somewhere that more marriages have been spoiled by bad breath than by infidelity. I live in terror of sour-smelling mouths, my own and those of others. Children of both sexes, young girls, and young cats can be approached without guile: no need to offer them mint candy, cigars, or garlic to mask the fetor of tired gums.

The whole of Montherlant's oeuvre validates, with Old Testament sternness, my forthcoming notice to lovelorn visitors. The only question is: Have I made my meaning plain? In a later, improved edition I may try a formula. Sexual interest of B in X (which we shall call I) is reduced in proportion to the amount by which the sexual interest of X in B exceeds the value of I. In my case it is not only sexual interest (and performance) that are so affected—the blight spreads over all of my affection for *X*. I cannot bear to receive more than I am able to give. Is this just my own starved and stingy heart, or are all males so constructed? (Montherlant is no help here; in his pages there is no love.)

WE MET AS AGREED on the second Thursday in April. I was jubilant about Carswell's defeat the day before and told Ben about how people we both knew had gone to Washington to lobby senators, for the first time in their lives, to bring about that result.

Carswell is so much worse than Haynsworth that we are lucky Nixon for once didn't get his revenge. Perhaps I should ask to be replaced in Paris and become a political agitator in New York like all my old friends. Do you think I've become respectable enough to fit in? It might suit me to get away from Pompidou and the agitators in France. I am tired of protesting shopkeepers!

Ben's suggesting, even in jest, that he might wish to return to New York was unexpected. I asked what was wrong. Had he failed to renew his sexual zoo?

Yes and no, he answered, I don't really know. I haven't paid very much attention.

He went on to explain that this was a dreary time for him. He had finished the work for the Oklahomans and now missed his bargaining sessions in Rabat with the president of the Moroccan company and the brilliant little Dr. Bensalem— exchanges at once intricate, tense, and suffused with friendship. For instance, he said, take the black bean soup and chef's salad they serve at your club. They're all right. But one look is enough to make me long for boiled mutton, chickpeas, couscous, and *harissa*, followed by a glass of mint tea. And for Moroccan waiters who start grinning as soon as you appear, shake your hand, and call you Chef. What I am working on in Paris is dull stuff: the sale of a family-owned French perfume manufacturer to the owners of an American cosmetics firm who are even richer. Their money is new. The deal is limping along in a setting worthy of a Buñuel. Our meetings are at the house of the matriarch of the tribe on avenue Foch. It has small sitting rooms that are perfect cubes, each with its own Impressionist masterpieces, where one can caucus between rounds of negotiations. Her butler passes stuffed eggs and whiskey and soda. Then we go in to lunch. The other week, I managed to extract from the old lady a piece of new information: Yes, now that I had reminded her, she thinks the family in fact owns—through "formalities"— those Swiss companies one has never heard of before that have recently turned up receiving most of the proceeds from the sale of their perfumes. Naturally, it's they and not the French company that have the rights to license the perfumes. No, the Swiss companies' books of account can't be revealed, let alone audited; a banker surely understands how important discretion and trust are in a family business. No, the family will not guarantee what those accounts might turn out to be; there are too many cousins to be consulted, the tax consequences might be unpleasant, she is no longer a young woman, one has to think of the worst.

How did this end? I asked him.

It hasn't. It can't. I have advised my clients to wait. As

soon as Madame Mère has her next attack of angina, which can't fail to come, the whole gang, including the family *notaire*, will be in such a funk over the French tax audit of the estate that they will agree to anything we ask, provided they receive ready funds that can end up in their numbered Swiss accounts.

In fact since early March, well before that visit, domestic arrangements no longer gave him comfort. Gianni's mother in Marseille was sick, probably dying. Ben told him to go there at once and look after her as long as was necessary; Madame Hamelin, the concierge, could bring the morning croissants and oranges and newspapers, make his bed, and do the laundry; he didn't want a temporary replacement, even if it was Gianni's best friend who had once worked for the Count de Vogüé. In the evenings, when he didn't have a dinner to go to—it seemed to him he was invited less than in the past, except, of course, to business affairs—often he did not get home until after the great charcuterie at the corner of the boulevard du Montparnasse had closed. But even if it was open, a paralyzing anguish he was not proud of stopped him from buying *oeufs en gelée*, pâté, and pickles, gripping a baguette of bread under his arm, and, so equipped, proceeding to a comfortable and solitary meal at the small table near the window from which he had a view on the garden. Was it that he did not want the amiable woman with rapid gestures who dispensed those items to rank him with the other men, so sour and careful, also waiting to buy their lonely supper? The days were becoming longer: he disliked thinking of the figure he might cut carrying a *filet* of provisions as he walked back toward the rue Férou.

The same disabling embarrassment made him shun restaurants where he was known and the grating solicitude of the headwaiters' inquiries: Will Monsieur dine alone or will "Madame"—which one, he wondered—be joining Monsieur later? The Coupole became his refuge; he could go there late, seek out the maître d'hôtel, who was his friend, mumble something about not having liked the play or having come directly from the airport, and order a full bottle of burgundy and grilled *andouille*—Ben liked, even in the worst of times, to eat always, in each restaurant he frequented, the one dish in which he believed it excelled. After a while, the roar of conversations surrounding him and the wine he had drunk induced a sense of tolerant detachment. When he saw an acquaintance pacing the aisles of the huge room in search of a table about to be vacated, usually someone who was not, like Ben, accustomed to being seated at once, he lowered his eyes to avoid recognition and comments on being alone. The waiter brought him a brandy and then another. The maître d'hôtel sometimes stopped by to complain about the pain in his feet. It would be well past midnight. Gently, the suppressed hope for an impending miracle—the woman with an expert mouth, painted the color of the plush banquette she leaned against, might fix him with her eyes and send a note suggesting they leave the restaurant together, or, like deus ex machina, a nearly forgotten college friend might suddenly hail him, a chic woman on each arm—turned into tipsy indifference.

Ben would walk back toward the rue du Cherche-Midi, past the middle-aged whores leaning against parked automobiles.

Across the boulevard glittered rue Vavin; within its short
span, the devastating, cold solitude of the hotels where one
could take them. In the other direction lay New Jimmy's.
What was the point? It was like dining with the Cockney:
revulsion at watching her eat followed by revulsion brought
on by repetitious exertions in bed and the new question their
encounters were posing. Would she again give him crabs?
The first onset of itching had puzzled him, as did the immobile
colorless dots among his pubic hairs. He borrowed tweezers
from Gianni and removed one of them for examination under
a bright light; the sight of the energetic, curled little legs
revived memories of lectures on this and related subjects
during basic training at Quantico. A pomade he acquired from
a scholarly pharmacist near the Madeleine—Ben thought the
neighborhood was appropriate for this sort of purchase—
proved highly effective. In the end, Ben decided that the best
policy was to repeat the treatments when necessary and let
the Cockney cling to the belief that her own puzzling itch,
which she mentioned with satisfaction, was but a natural
manifestation of her desire for Ben and the expanding group
of men producing the same effect. Discussing the affliction,
eventually sharing the pomade with her, seemed risky: it
could be taken either as an invitation to greater familiarity or
as a humiliating reproof, like the boorish effort he had once
made to correct her table manners. On the other hand, if he
asked that she shave, like her friend Marianne, he risked
adding flame to her already excessive fervor. Was he an udder
attached to a garrulous milking machine?

At home, he watched over his supply of Black Label scotch,

ordering it from the Nicolas at the rue de Sèvres by the half case. He believed he shouldn't go to the Coupole too often. What would the waiters imagine? Would the way he dressed, his neatly barbered appearance, the generous tips he left, and his choice of good wine save him from demotion, or would he become one of the regulars—men and women found at the Coupole and the Lipp evening after evening, behind the same little table, glasses automatically set before them and refilled, reading *Le Monde* or staring blankly, dining off Baltic herring? It was the charcuterie dilemma posed in slightly different terms.

Guy Renard had a new girl, with whom he had not yet slept; he was either not going to parties or not offering to take Ben along. Once those parties had been Ben's chief amusement. Ben still waited daily for Guy's telephone call; sometimes it reached him at the office, frequently a good bit later, at home, when he had already had a couple of whiskeys, taken a bath, and half decided on the evening's dreary course. Guy would propose dinner, just the three of them, but first a scotch at Ben's. Guy talked and Ben poured. The girl stood with her back to the fire, submissive long legs within reach of Guy's hand; he caressed her like a horse. The bistro was usually somewhere on the other side of Paris. Guy would drive, careening around corners, taking shortcuts up wrong way streets. They left the car on the sidewalk, carelessly; parking tickets were still cheap in Paris and could be fixed by practically anyone. They drank at table, afterward at Paprika, where there were gypsies, and again at Ben's. Ben knew that Guy needed an audience and that the audience bored the girl; he was tired of being that audience; he didn't want the friendship to wear out; his own boredom was hard to re-press—at times he would offer Guy and the girl a drink when they arrived and in a short while ask them to leave. He would invent a subsequent engagement of his own, with which one of the beautiful Americans he knew so well? Ben would not say. This was, Ben thought, as good a way to maintain his independence and social authority as any other. Before departing for Marseille, Gianni had prepared a vast store of Dutch cheese crackers and macadamia nuts. When finally alone, Ben raided that store, replenished the ice in the bucket, and drank and read until he fell asleep over his book.

He was rereading *The Notebooks of Malte Laurids Brigge*. Years ago, in the course of a boisterous meal, he had recommended that text, located so strangely between dream and Rilke's recollections, as a cure for my nostalgia for Paris and certain other places I had known in Europe; he said I was suffering from unseemly illusions about what might have been, typical in a henpecked husband. It is true that I had been jealous of his constantly popping over to Paris or London or, for that matter, to Sydney and Tokyo, lingering there, amassing impressions and anecdotes, while I trudged up Madison Avenue to take the children to school, down Madison Avenue to the magazine, and then back up the same route for our early family dinner.

Read the *Notebooks*, he said, you will see what Paris is really like when you are alone, your work, like some acrobat's performance finally over, and you have let down your guard—perhaps because you are tired, perhaps because you are sad. Uncertainty and fear ooze out of walls of buildings, out of the walls of your elegant hotel room, even if the housekeeper has remembered to put the standard bouquet of roses and carnations with the director's compliments on the desk next to the room-service menu and laundry lists. You drift past houses, along boulevards, like a blank piece of paper.

Of course, he added, in prescribing *Malte* I assume that you are sufficiently neurotic, which is as yet unproved. The best treatment for other cases of sedentary wanderlust is to meditate on original sin and the dreary ubiquity of evil—if you don't believe me, then read Baudelaire's "Le Voyage"!

Ben was not always able to keep literary references or analogies in check, so that a book that held his attention had a way of infiltrating his daily life. In consequence, his fixation on the *Notebooks* during the spring of 1970 was probably unfortunate. If challenged or if his mood changed, he would have been quick enough to point out the preposterous imperfections of the analogy hinted at. Like Malte, he was sad and lonely, but he was not helpless or racked by fever—I would have added, perhaps mistakenly but with some considerable confidence, that his depressions were not very frequent. In any case, the elegant house he rented from my cousin Olivia was as different as possible from the dingy furnished room the destitute Danish nobleman inhabited in the rue Toullier; when Ben, his manservant being absent, with his own hands, to take the chill off the spring evening, lit the fire his respectable concierge had laid in the splendid fireplace and helped himself to another drink, the scene had only the search for warmth to connect it with the smoking iron stove in a fifth-story room where weary Malte must force himself to rest his head on his armchair, "for there is a certain greasy-grey hollow in its green covering, into which all heads seem to fit." Nor did Ben have to slink into a *crémerie* for a frugal meal or dream of having enough money to eat at Duval's— a chain of restaurants now defunct that Ben would have disdained to enter. Nevertheless, when Ben, for his own reasons, stayed away from the Coupole and dined on junk food and whiskey instead of striding joyously into all the restaurants where he would have been welcome as a valued habitué, Malte was at his side, and it was Malte who perched timorously at the edge of the leather seat, hands gripped white with tension, when Ben actually took out his car to run an errand or make a visit in some neighborhood where using a taxi would have been too irrationally inconvenient or because, as often happened, a taxi simply could not be found. For Ben was suffering again from that irritating inability to steer his car that had afflicted him when he first settled in Paris. He considered consulting a Parisian "alienist," but the vision of Malte in his "tolerably decent suit" among the doctors of the neurological ward of the Salpêtrière provided a literary, and therefore acceptable, reason for delay; to satisfy his practical side, he also thought that, when Gianni returned, he might ask him to drive or engage a chauffeur.

Sometime in April, Ben received an invitation to a party the Decazes were giving on the second Saturday in May. There was to be dancing; he supposed it was their major social effort of the year. Without giving much thought to whether he would in fact attend, Ben told his secretary to accept and was surprised that Paul nevertheless telephoned him twice to make sure that nothing had gone amiss, and they could count on his finally coming to their house.

Excerpts from Notaben 298, dated 8/5/70:

Friday night. Across America, young couples going out, receiving friends, feeling left out if they don't. Single, lonely men and women and old people hide in their rooms. On weekends or vacations in the country, Rachel and I would keep our ear to the ground: Are the Abthorps not giving their Fourth of July picnic this year or have they not asked us? And the Parkers and the Smiths? These questions we sometimes put to each other, for instance, after the third drink, or when we had just made love and it was easy to say how much better that was than doing X, Y, or Z, or when Rachel was writing down the list of whom we might invite to dinner. Was there anyone to whom we "owed"? But the real question was left unuttered: Have we become a couple so awful that no one can have us? We enter a house and the milk curdles, the phonograph needle scratches the Louis Armstrong record, the nursemaid runs screaming back to Ireland. . . .

Perhaps not this Friday night. All the right dinner parties have been canceled: the hostess is on a bus to Washington in her tie-dyed T-shirt and sandals, to protest Kent State and the "incursion." If they are lucky, Ron Ziegler may deliver himself of another

pronouncement about the forces of history. The
nation shakes with shame and fury. "Incursion" is
such an elegant and precise word: in the military
context, it means a hostile inroad or invasion, esp.
one of sudden and hasty character, a sudden attack. In
other contexts, its use can strike one as quite droll.
For instance, Dr. Johnson's "The inevitable incursion
of new images." I verified this in the *OED*, struck by
wonder that these Nixon people had such a thing in
their vocabulary. Of course, they say "incursion"
because they want to make invading Cambodia sound
like a light, temporary activity, almost gay and frothy;
invasion has a different texture and connotation—like
Hitler marching into Poland or Napoleon into Russia.
Long time, lots of dead people, quite the wrong
image. But I am beating about the bush to avoid
declaring here, in the cozy privacy of Olivia's study,
whether I too would have taken the bus or train with
the young Abthorps—or old Olivia. You bet she is
there; probably spending the night with Joe Alsop!
Never let politics get in the way of having a good
dinner and catching up on gossip, that's what I say.
The fact is that I would have gone—in some other
direction!—for instance to Tokyo, like in October '68.
Signing petitions, letting one's name appear in
newspaper advertisements, helping pay for those
advertisements, are all very well, but a sensitive
nature shrinks from the promiscuity of
demonstrations; one's vocal chords are too tender for

all that shouting and chanting. Leave it to the
wellborn hippies—Sarah and Rebecca and Prudence
and Cousin Olivia; they have the common touch.

Besides, when you come right down to it, who am
I to explain to Gov. Rhodes how to run the great
state of Ohio? He would listen to one sentence and
ask me what country I come from!

Question: Isn't Malte lucky to be able to recollect
all those family ghosts—punctually appearing in
pompous dining rooms or at the far end of some
greensward—and have all those dropsical
chamberlains and melancholy masters of the hunt to
think about, even while he has the heebie-jeebies
wondering about Paris? These visions add up to a
lace-collar, heavy-cream Danish childhood. My
visions are unmentionable or have been blotted out.
I am less daffy, but have nothing. I am like Tarzan,
a droll apeman who missed a boyhood, but I don't
know how to swing from tree to tree or be loved
by Jane.

Tomorrow is Paul and Véronique's fete. If I go, I
will get to hear the assembled *avocats* and *notaires* of
Passy explain to me the finer points of military
strategy. You would think there is not one of them
who did not learn realpolitik at Henry Kissinger's
own knee. It's nice though that everybody here thinks
of me as *le gentil américain*.

The note of which this is a part is exceptionally long and
digressive—I suppose he was up most of the night, the bottle

and ice within easy reach—containing, in addition to material about Véronique, a hodgepodge of literary allusions interspersed with remarks on the correct pricing and distribution of Scandinavian state bonds and reports of developments concerning a certain Agnès who shampooed Ben's hair at Desfossé's celebrated establishment before Monsieur Bruno would cut it. It appears that Agnès had not been unaware of the effect her legs and other anatomical characteristics had on her client or of the charm of Ben's wit when he discoursed in the barber chair (which charm was accentuated by the generosity of the *petit cadeau* he pressed into her warm, soft hand upon departing). She showed her gratitude by letting her bosom rest against Ben's shoulder while she massaged his scalp and her intelligence by announcing, so that Ben could hear but Monsieur Bruno could not, that on Thursdays after work she usually took tea on the terrace of Fouquet's. The rest, Ben found, was easy, especially as Agnès had no ambition to introduce Ben into her social life or to enter his (such as it was).

The next morning, May 9, he rose late, opened the window, and felt the air. It was a warm day. He thought of driving to the park in Saint-Cloud, going for a walk in the long shady alley that leads to the Rond de Chasse, so often deserted even on a spring weekend, and then returning to lunch off dry sausage, eggs with mayonnaise, and sardines under a chestnut tree at the *guinguette* near the Balustrade. I knew the place. He had taken Prudence and me there during our visit; although the season was over, surprisingly we found the place open; the small room adjoining the kitchen, never used in season, was heated by a fireplace. We had noticed that the waitress set these very dishes and a bottle of Rhône wine on the table without being asked. It was apparently Ben's normal fare. They had engaged in a conversation I had been able to follow only partially—about the woman's daughter, who had unaccountably left her job, perhaps in that very establishment, although her marriage was delayed because the fiancé had been laid off, and the woman's leg, which, judging by the way she limped, was badly in need of repair. It made one feel guilty to be sitting at the table while she lurched back and forth from the counter bringing the bottle of Evian Prudence asked for, the *cornichons* she had forgotten, and cold chicken after Ben finally inquired whether there was anything different we might like to eat.

But this Saturday morning, he was slow getting started and slow reading about Cambodia in the newspapers. By the time he was ready, it was past noon. He vacillated about getting dressed: if he was really going to Saint-Cloud, cotton trousers and a sweater were enough; on the other hand he disliked not wearing a necktie in the city, which meant he should wear a coat, which in turn made him lean toward flannels. He calculated how long it would take to cross Paris by car if he took the avenue de Versailles, and the countervailing risk of delay by construction work if he stuck to the Left Bank quays. Then he realized that he could not count on taking his walk and still getting a meal at the *guinguette*— they would have run out of bread or meat or coffee—and that to drive all the way there and afterward have to look for lunch in Paris would spoil the pleasure of the outing. He walked instead along the rue de Vaugirard to the Luxembourg Garden, watched the tennis disdainfully—it seemed the

French had a congenital learning disability when it came to that game—and, later, children sailing boats. The woman who rented them to children was there; a fresh little breeze made the boats heel and then gracefully come about; a wave of personal unhappiness mixed with joy at the sight of what seemed to be the happiness of others—the nicely dressed children and their nicely dressed parents, so pleasantly united, addressing civilized remonstrances one to another—overcame Ben. He sat down on one of the green iron chairs. This was not unlike the boat pond in Central Park, except that the boats were fancier than the ones he had given to the twins; many were remote-controlled. He considered briefly the unlikely prospect of buying such a toy for himself, and a beret, and joining the group of experts, retired postal employees, he surmised, who were busy with some very serious racing.

His mood changed; he paid for his seat and headed for lunch at the Lipp. The place was still crowded—fortunately, Ben thought, it's not Sunday; one need not stare at divorced fathers feeding steak and *frites* to bored offspring—but the owner's nephew who stood guard that day led him to a table in the back room. Ben welcomed the cool after the walk. The indifferent boiled beef was what he had expected. He drank his bottle of wine and, realizing the emptiness of the rest of the day, ordered an eau-de-vie. The nephew was already having his own solitary lunch at the accustomed table. Ben paid the bill, got into a taxi, and drove home.

It was dark when he woke from his nap. He remembered that he was to go to the Decazes and his previous perplexity at an annoying aspect of their invitation: it was for ten-thirty, but they had not invited him to dinner. That was fair enough if one lived near Arpajon, but why did they expect him to travel all the way from Paris if there was nothing for him to do until that hour? In the event, he didn't mind; it was already close to ten, but he considered it normal that, if the hostess had not asked one to dine at her house before a dance, she should arrange to have someone living nearby do it. Could it be that they did not seriously expect him—he found that difficult to reconcile with Paul's officious telephone reminders—or did different rules prevail in the region between Fontainebleau and Rambouillet? It was also odd that Guy Renard had not telephoned. If Paul and Véronique intended to make a show of politeness, a reasonable hypothesis, given Paul's avidity—the word was not too strong—for the assignments Ben caused to come his way, then the correct thing was to invite their mutual friend also. In that case, one might have thought Guy would have said either that he had accepted or that he would not be seeing Ben at the party. On the other hand, it was true that it was some time since Ben had last heard Guy mention the beautiful Odile and the Montorgueil château. Perhaps the answer to this puzzle was that Guy was no longer welcome at the Decazes' neighbors and Véronique had found it more tactful not to have him at her party. Inductive reasoning produced no answer to these questions. Ben decided to dress and make his way to the Decazes', if indeed he was able to understand the directions they had sent. He would look over the situation at the party from the outside, and thus deduce the correct answer and what further action he should take.

By the time he had opened the street gate with the aid of Madame Hamelin's husband, maneuvered the car in reverse gear out of the courtyard and through the porte cochère, rushed back upstairs to get the forgotten directions from his dressing room, and was finally navigating toward the Porte d'Orléans, real night had fallen. Ben turned on the radio and found the news. A crowd of a hundred thousand (was it possible?)—Norman Mailer and other representative great Americans among them—had marched on the White House. But, previous to that, by the dawn's early light, Nixon had held a meeting with students at the Lincoln Memorial, and no harm came to either side; was a new age of miracles about to begin?

The need for an immediate decision interrupted his meditation. He had thought he knew how to reach Corbeil, which was not far from Arpajon. Should he stop to look at the map or rely on right reason? His sense of adventure prevailed: essentially, it was like going past Orly, only a little different; before or after Corbeil, he would turn west, probably after following some sign to Centre Ville. He realized that he had forgotten to have a drink before setting out and that it was many hours since lunch. Also, he was going too fast, but if he slowed down, other drivers on this three-lane highway passed him unpleasantly, as though intent on penetrating his anus as well as his car trunk, and, for good measure, blinding him before they darted, klaxons blaring, toward the headlights of an approaching car. It was better to stay ahead of them. Chalky villages and towns appeared and vanished; the streets were deserted; sooner than expected, he saw a monument to the World War I dead and the sign that said he had entered Corbeil.

Now Ben pulled over to the side of the road and rummaged

in the glove compartment. The flashlight battery was dead or the thing simply refused to work. In the light of the overhead lamp he examined the Decaze directions: there was no mention of Corbeil; they had assumed one would be coming through Rambouillet, which he realized was nowhere near; inexplicably, the road map was not in its accustomed place; guided by right reason he decided to head in the direction of Chartres and hope for the best.

Creamy fog in orderly rolls like barbed wire intermittently cut the road; it rose in barricades on both sides. Ben liked to motor in conditions of adversity. He turned on his fog lights, rejoicing in the yellow hues they imparted to the night. Arpajon! He had made it; it remained to find the village immediately beyond, then the Decazes' manoir or whatever else it might turn out to be. Another roadside stop revealed the remainder of the problem. Not only was the basic approach to Arpajon organized for drivers coming from Rambouillet, but so were the more arcane instructions. The fog thickened. According to the car clock, it was almost midnight. Ben was hungry. A great wish to floor the gas pedal and rush back to Paris and the welcoming arms of the headwaiter at the Coupole came upon him. He decided to give the Decazes another five minutes, and they had almost lost when abruptly, on the right, an arrow appeared, indicating a communal road— hardly a road at all—to Montlhéry. That name figured in the directions, just the sort of slight hint that the trained mind of a reserve marine officer needed to solve a problem on patrol.

In the interval between two banks of fog he made out a shape on the right that could indeed be a château, with its obligatory wall and multiple entrances for different grades of visitors. That would be the Montorgueil place. He drove to the end of the wall: again to the right, between ditches and rows of willows on either side, was a track wide enough for a car; presumably, he was again following a wall of the Montorgueil property. Another two hundred meters, yet another entrance to the right and, at last, a ridiculously long row of parked cars. He drove to the head of it; he had arrived; in Michelin terms, it remained to be seen whether what awaited him could justify the voyage.

There was light in every window in the house. Torches burned in iron holders outside the door. The undistinguished form of this brick building and the modern look of the bricks made Ben suppose it had been originally intended to lodge the *régisseur* or a relative with a disputed title claim to part of the property. On one side lay structures that might be stables or carriage barns. On the other, attached to the house, was a glass hothouse also glowing with light. There was no point in tugging on the bellpull. He opened the moist front door and, eyes blinking, entered the house. Paul was at the end of the hall, with a group of florid men wearing evening clothes a size or two too small; as he came forward to greet Ben, he raised his arms in a gesture that could imply thanksgiving or despair. They had given up hope of seeing him; Véronique was in the conservatory; drinks were in the dining room he would pass on his way, so was the Camembert and probably also Guy Renard; dancing was to the right. Indeed, the thud of feet shifting to the beat of the monkey came from that direction. Ben heard the florid men say their last names; either he was right, and they were all of them *notaires*, or Paul had assembled skilled impersonators. Ben gave both his names, on principle, *à l'américaine*, and rapidly decided it was time to move on in search of drink, food, and my cousin Véronique.

She was wearing a long dress of very dark green pleated silk. Her arms were bare, thin, and, for this season, extraordinarily white. When he bowed to kiss her hand—she was perching, on the edge of a large cement tub planted with white flowers, alongside another young woman he did not recognize—he smelled her perfume. It seemed heavy for someone her age and had been liberally applied. Véronique addressed him in French: the young woman was Lavinia, Paul's unmarried half sister who worked for French *Vogue*. They had been in the same convent school; she had met Paul at Lavinia's house; they were best friends. A man passed with a tray of drinks; Ben asked if he could have two whiskeys, one for immediate consumption and one to nurse when he had finished. They laughed. Véronique said he had better sit down beside them, a man so thirsty must be tired. He even looked tired. They would take care of him. All Americans liked Virginia ham. Lavinia would bring him a plate. Now that Véronique had at last lured him into her private jungle she would not let him get away. Ben wondered if her dress was by Fortuny. She put her hand on his shoulder—the gesture surprised Ben—and said he was right: her American grandfather, Jack's great-uncle, had taken long to recover from his wounds; endless months of the convalescence were spent in Venice. At the time, he was rich and bought a number of these dresses for his wife, whom she, Véronique, resembled. Her own mother was short and round. It was lucky her mother had not sold them. Now they all belonged to her. She asked if he knew how one rolled these sheaths into serpents of silk to put them away in a drawer or into a suitcase. But they made her feel she was a serpent, they were her skin. Had he thought, she asked, about how there was nothing between a serpent and its skin, and yet the serpent sheds it?

Lavinia returned and so did the man with drinks. Véronique asked him to put a bottle of whiskey and a bottle of soda and some ice beside them. She stretched her arms before her and said she was tired of the party and her other guests; Paul could look after them. After all, except for Lavinia and Ben they were Decaze friends. It occurred to Ben that my family's drinking genes had been transmitted by my great-uncle Hugh to Véronique and more mysteriously to Lavinia—or was it the result of a Vassar education in the case of Véronique and of the frequentation of Condé Nast colleagues in the case of the sister-in-law? They asked him to tell his life story. Paul claimed Ben was a man with a mysterious past he did not like to reveal. In fact, telling the story of his life at parties was not Ben's preferred occupation. He decided that the abridged, ironic version would do. As always, it was like hearing another man speak. They said he must write a book; had he read *The Painted Bird*? Ben replied he had, as soon as it was published; it was one of the reasons why he was proof against literary temptations that might distract him from making money. What about their lives? Lavinia pouted—before she was eighteen, it was all about how to lose her virginity, now it was about how to find a decent apartment for less than five hundred dollars a month.

And Véronique? Lavinia already knows the story, replied Véronique, I will tell it to you only if you ask me to lunch or dinner.

Lavinia interrupted, saying, He can't do that, Paul is much too jealous.

Once more he heard Véronique laugh—a cascade of triumphant sound. Ben thought he would never forget it. Miraculously, it lifted his spirits. He felt things might go better in some form he could not yet recognize.

But he can do it when Paul is away, she said, turning to Lavinia. Don't you know that he will be sailing during the Pentecostal weekend and the following week as well? Ben can't possibly know it. Paul likes clients to think he never leaves the office.

Later, on his way to say good-bye to Paul—it seemed he would have to make an effort to look for him, the group in the entrance hall having dissolved probably long ago—Ben saw Guy on a low sofa in the corner of a room, half dining room and half library, where the bar was set up. He was speaking with habitual intensity to a girl Ben didn't know. Perhaps it was the obliging Odile. Thinking it might be discreet not to give a sign of recognition, Ben concentrated all his attention on the hunting scene above the sideboard and was about to exit, feigning distraction, when he heard Guy's deep, courteous and teasing baritone: At last the only elegant American in Paris has appeared, one who qualifies as American only because his list of good addresses in Paris is better than any Parisian's. Guy wanted to know where Ben had gone in the morning. He had called, he said, in the hope they would drive out to the Decazes' together, stopping for dinner on the way, in Rambouillet, at the Maison des Champs, with an after-dinner pause at the house of Odile's aunt next door. Did Ben have plans for lunch, in just a few hours? They would pick him up; he was sure to know a bistro that was open on Sunday.

For no particular reason, thanking Paul for the party had begun to seem less necessary. Ben found his car with some difficulty. There was nobody there to see him; he urinated against a bush. Before he reached the highway, the fog had lifted and the sky was streaked with light. Those two beautiful young women had found him interesting—there might be more to it than that. They were of a milieu he thought he understood. Although drunk, he had done nothing to botch it; he had, in fact, behaved well. He could, if he wanted, hear Véronique's crystal laughter again.

Looking at the brightening sky, he remembered a coming-out party in Bar Harbor for the Parkers' third daughter. The night had been unusually mild. On the way to the Parkers' from a prefatory dinner, there was a violent scene with Rachel. She had shrieked, opened the car door just as he was accelerating into a long curve, threatened to jump out. It related somehow to money. When they finally arrived at the party, his hands were trembling. Rachel went into the house—to dance? to get away from him? He stayed outside, talked for a while with portly, beautifully shaved Charlie Parker, face pink above his white tie, beaming at the guests and his own prosperity, and then sat down on the stone edge of a raised flower bed near the side porch and listened to the orchestra work its way through Irving Berlin. The eldest daughter, Maggie, passed by, asked him to dance, and when he declined wanted to know what was the matter. He said he was unhappy. She sat down beside him. They remained there until it was almost dawn; after a while, she held his hand. Then Rachel, as though nothing had happened, came out of the house and announced she was tired—it was time to take her home. So he gave Maggie a kiss on the cheek and trudged off across the lawn to get the station wagon. Life went on in its preset way. There was no need for that now. At least he was free to set his own course.

He returned to Paris through Corbeil, as he had come— why look for Rambouillet at this hour? The road seemed miraculously short. When he arrived at the corner of Montparnasse and the rue de Vaugirard, where he decided he would leave the car instead of struggling with the gate, Ben saw that the metal curtain of the *épicerie* had been cranked halfway up; the owner was on the sidewalk outside, prying apart with a hammer the slats of a crate of bananas. Ben bought two and ate them at once, voraciously. They would stave off his hangover. He threw the peels into a basket filled with discarded lettuce leaves and onions.

IV

TWO DAYS LATER, on the Monday after that weekend of exultation, I telephoned Ben to tell him that my daughters and I had marched in Washington—Prudence was sick with a bad throat—linking arms with strangers, singing at the top of our voices, and also to ask whether he could get away from Paris over the Memorial Day holiday and join us in Vermont. I said he didn't need to fear landing in the midst of one of our family reunions. It would be just the five of us, lots of bad tennis, and no organized activities. For once, in a matter of this kind, Ben did not chill me with his "European" point of view. He understood what was happening in America. The French television had played clips of the march; he had watched them on Sunday. As for the visit I proposed, he said he would try to come but couldn't make any plans. The office was busier than ever. Then he told me he had been to the Decazes' party.

You see the effect of living in different time zones, he said. Events never coincide. While you were still marching I might have been on the dance floor. Instead I talked to Véronique. That was a momentous occasion in its own way. It's possible that thanks to you I am now in a more cheerful landscape.

In fact, when Ben looked back on it during the days that followed, Véronique's flirtatious manner and what he took to be a proposal that he invite her in her husband's absence troubled him. They seemed too bold and provocative for the circumstances, but he wasn't sure his assessment was correct. Possibly it was nothing more than a high-spirited way of ending a long and too personal conversation that had begun to bore her. Something akin to the way she laughed. That her husband's half sister had been present supported this interpretation. But, on the other hand, wasn't Lavinia's presence a cover of which Véronique skillfully took advantage rather than a constraint? The latter interpretation was reinforced by Ben's conviction that a current of sorts had surged between them when he described his paltry wartime miseries—could it be that "She lov'd me for the dangers I had pass'd"?—as it had earlier when, unexpectedly, she had touched his arm. But if she was attracted to him and tempted by the prospect of an adventure, should he not avoid involvement with this temperamental married woman?

Ben's dislike of entanglements, and a closely allied consideration—his reluctance to have disorders of his personal life seep into the neat, protected space in which he conducted official business, the bank's and his own—were deeply rooted. The Cockney, Dolores, and her shipowner husband did not count—he considered them commedia dell'arte figures and dealt with them accordingly—but although he hardly knew Véronique or Paul, she was my cousin and a "nice" woman, mother of a five-year-old boy and wife of an equally "nice" man. Why should Ben let his shadow pass over their happiness? In addition, according to all reports, the legal work Paul was doing for Ben's firm was valuable. He had in a sense become a part of the office, and Ben despised office romances as threatening to discipline, objectivity, and concentration on servicing the interests of the bank. During the period immediately following his separation from Rachel, when friends' wives like so many curious social workers rushed to care for this elusive, strangely correct, and wounded man, he had scrupulously declined offers of solace from spouses of partners and junior colleagues—those offers so often communicated by the lady's surprising substitution of a moist kiss on the lips for the previous handshake or chaste peck on the cheek.

Ben held sleeping with the wives of close friends to be a riskless and potentially beneficial activity from the point of view of all concerned. His own discretion was total—he never revealed a single name even to me, only the process. As for the straying wife, he thought one could normally count on her distaste for scandal, especially if she had small children and if one explained in advance, as he never failed to, that one's affection for good old Greg or Sam and determination not to marry again were equally unshakable. Ben insisted to me that in fact there was never any difficulty: he had simply gotten to understand and like better a number of our mutual friends and their families; the drain on his finances was negligible—frequent outings to chic restaurants, weekends in London or Acapulco, and presents of jewelry all being obviously ruled out. Since ignorance is bliss, it was not necessary to take the husband's perspective on these doings into account. But, when he did, Ben concluded that the husband came out ahead. In the worst of hypotheses, Ben's sexual performance made the hitherto undervalued husband look better. If, on the contrary, the lady was satisfied, she returned to the nuptial couch relaxed, possibly with more positive ideas about what might be attained there. But the existence of office or professional links changed all that; in the particular case of the Decazes, the lack of a shared history of friendship that would dispose the lady to collaborate in the preservation of general good order made for a volatility, for unpredictable potential disruptions of family and business relations. Worse, it would make demands on Ben's time and involve him in systematic lying.

Whether Ben believed in these lunchtime theories, and to what extent they reflected his experience, I wasn't sure. But each time he expounded them, I was grateful he did not feel it necessary to assure me that Prudence and I were not included in their ambit. As I noted at the outset, Ben liked paradoxes in conversation. He had a similar (albeit more superficial) propensity to contradictions in his daily behavior. Among them were the way in which he shied from attachments, although he suffered from loneliness, and how he lied with gusto if asked where he had dined the previous evening or whether he liked Tchaikovsky and yet strenuously avoided situations requiring sustained falsehood.

There was another wholly different reason for him to vacillate. Dolores had just written suggesting that he spend that same Pentecostal weekend in Athens. The work on her new house in Kifisiá was finished; the husband had business in New York; Ben could stay at the Grande Bretagne and go to the museum in the morning. "We will have lunch in Piraeus with broiled fish. All afternoon you will love me," she concluded. Ben was tempted. So it happened that a note of thanks to Véronique for the evening in Arpajon came close to marking, for the time being, the end of his contact with my cousin. True, there was no necessity to go to Athens on that particular weekend in order to enjoy such uncomplicated pleasures. Dolores's husband was often away: Ben thought he could tell her that he too was going to New York (lest she come to Paris or offer to meet him in whatever other city he named as his destination). On the other hand, right then Dolores might help him keep black thoughts at bay, while later in the summer he might be over his depression and, in any case, Athens would be too hot.

Yet Véronique's offer had a peremptory quality. It had to be taken up right then or not at all. And what would Véronique think if he ignored it? That he had not understood her or was timorous—or, possibly, that he had found her unattractive? Each of these suppositions and others like them, in addition to being untrue, implied an undeserved insult to her or a loss of face for him. His memory was vivid of how she had looked at the cocktail party at the rue du Cherche-Midi and then in the Fortuny dress in her own house, and of the peculiar old-fashioned perfume that progressively combined with the nascent delicate odor of her sweat. It had been warm in the conservatory; she had perspired; probably she used no powder or deodorants, just little dots of that perfume. Desire for Véronique, brutal and urgent, made itself felt. He should invite her, he thought, to a restaurant where the food and wine were good and the decor refined enough to go naturally with an elegant woman—at the same time, although Paris in principle would have been emptied for Pentecost of everyone but tourists—it was better, so that she need not feel nervous, to avoid places where people she knew were likely to dine. Was this his punishment? he wondered. Was he condemned to pore over restaurant guides and wine lists like Sisyphus rolling his rock uphill?

He put down the papers he had been studying, dialed the number himself, and arranged to see her on Friday evening of the weekend she had named; he wanted the entire time Paul was absent to be open before them. He asked that she meet him at Ledoyen, in one of the gardens of the Champs-Élysées. Her voice was tiny and colorless. She said yes.

ON THE FRIDAY he was finally to see her, he went home after the office—Paris was indeed deserted, the taxi ride took less than ten minutes—bathed, washed his hair for the second time that day, clipped his fingernails and toenails, and dressed with extreme care. His newest black shoes seemed dull. He buffed them himself, telling Gianni to rush to the florist's before she closed, to make sure that the flowers in the house were fresh, and to change his sheets and the towels in his bathroom. He decided he would leave his car with the door-man of the Crillon. From there he walked to the restaurant, hardly conscious of the red and yellow flower beds, then at the height of their glory, carefully staying on the pavement so that the dust of the garden *allée* would not whiten his gleaming shoes.

He was precisely on time. The red-plush foyer was empty; some people were in the bar. He decided to wait for her at the table—it would be at least five minutes—to avoid the awkwardness of greeting her at the door and then crossing the dining room at the side of a young woman who was still a stranger. Was she not a little taller than he? He supposed she would wear very high heels. Also, he wanted to make sure of the table. It was a table at the window and it was all right; they could turn their backs on the other diners and face the mass of green outside. The garden lights had just been turned on; the green was changing to a Magritte navy blue.

This time her hair was down, not quite to her shoulders, gathered loosely by a ribbon that ended in an enamel clasp above her forehead. Ben found it less becoming than the chignon she had worn on the two previous occasions: her features, typical of a blond, floating just a little, changeable, needed a touch of severity or concentration; he regretted that her ears were covered. She was a little out of breath, as though she had been running, and her chest moved heavily under a dress of red crepe de chine with a pattern of smug, cream-colored Buddhas. Ben told her she was very beautiful. She laughed, asked if he was surprised that she had kept the engagement, and when he replied—truthfully—that he had never doubted it, laughed again and said he was odiously sure of himself. The reason she was late and had not had time to put up her hair, she informed him, was that she had decided only twenty minutes before to meet him. Until then, she had planned to call the restaurant and say her car had broken down. That would not have worked, Ben said; he would have sent his own car for her. She then told him, in possible contradiction, that she had arranged to stay in town: her mother-in-law agreed to invite Laurent (that was her son's name) and the au pair for the weekend.

She ate and drank fast, almost rapaciously; in contrast to the impression given at the party by the pallor of her arms, she seemed to him admirably wholesome. He said it was time for the life story she had promised. She asked him to wait until after dessert; she couldn't both talk and pay attention to food.

After she had finished her sherbet, she told the story, at first almost as woodenly, Ben thought, as he had told his own in Arpajon. The anecdotal part that concerned my great-uncle and my family, of course, he knew; she had loved horses, still did, thought she could handle any steeplechase course; she jumped with her legs open, it was all in the balance, it had been awful to leave for Vassar and give up racing and now they couldn't afford to keep a good horse and, anyway, Paul wanted her to be in Paris during the week. There was a pause during which she peered into the mirror of her compact. Then she continued: I changed my mind about Vassar very soon. All those friends of Jack's on weekends—I kept on falling in love. I even wanted to marry Jack, but he paid no attention. He said I was his little sister. Would that have stopped you? All those gods and pharaohs liked it, and I would have met you so much sooner!

For the second time, the recklessness of my cousin's conversation disconcerted Ben. Was she acceding to his wishes before they had taken form? Why had she named me? This was a door he preferred not to open. Like a man steering into a long skid, he mumbled in English that yes, vice is nice but incest is best. She smiled. Her compact occupied her again.

Knowing from me that the father was dead, Ben asked about Véronique's mother. This was the way to steer the conversation onto a road that was circuitous but left him in control. Where he wanted that road to lead he hadn't yet decided.

The flat truthfulness of her answer surprised me when I read his notes. She said she drove on occasional weekends to her mother's place because she wanted Laurent to know the house where she had grown up, but it was difficult for her to be with her mother alone: her mother had beat her and continued to do so even when she was in college and came home on vacations. She hit her with a riding whip—they were always around—or a clothes hanger or an umbrella, whatever was near. Véronique would have great welts and black-and-blue marks on her back and legs.

Horrified, Ben asked why she had put up with it, especially once she was no longer a child. Véronique answered that she was not sure she any longer knew the answer. At the time, it had seemed to her that the beatings calmed her mother and made things go better in the house for a while—her mother was extremely nervous, perhaps hysterical—besides, she had gotten used to it. She didn't mind the hurt, just that it showed, because she always had to remember when she shouldn't be seen undressed.

That's probably why I married Paul, she added carelessly. When I graduated from Vassar, I was looking for a job in Paris, but I would go home to the country on Saturdays, and my mother was still beating me. I met Paul in Paris, at Lavinia's birthday party. He took me out afterward, and we went to the room I had in a friend's apartment on the rue Jacob. We made love with all our clothes on, even my underpants. Fortunately he wanted it that way; I could not have let him see my body. And then? Then he asked to marry me and I told my mother and she said I was lucky, he is so solid, and she stopped hitting me. We had Laurent, and my mother gave me the money to buy an apartment and a house in the country, and now he usually takes me undressed.

Her eyes were empty—Ben wondered whether the earlier impression of health and freshness was misleading, perhaps she was, in fact, a little mad, or whether there were other things she was thinking of, had been on the verge of saying, and then had decided she would not speak about. She was playing with a lump of sugar on the table. Without thinking, Ben covered her hand with his. It was a warm, quiet hand; he realized that his own was cold as ice and that he was trembling. It doesn't matter, she said, it has all turned out pretty well. My mother also liked to ride. She taught me herself, when I was little. If I had a horse now, I would still be good; I could ride in any terrain. They drank a brandy, and then another. Véronique smiled. Now it was she who took his hand. She said she was curious whether Ben was really tenderhearted, tender like a woman, or afraid of his own thoughts.

He said he was afraid. In the town where he lived at the beginning of the war, when the Germans first came, there was a friend of his parents'—a large, blond woman, with permanent lazy cheerfulness. He remembered her wearing shiny silk blouses that stretched tight over a bosom which like everything else about her—arms, lips, even her back— was surprisingly ample. When she bent down to kiss him, he would try to peek at her breasts. The valley between them was also oversized and smelled sweet of powder. One day, the Germans took her to the Gestapo or SS house. She was kept there one night, perhaps two. He no longer remembered why they took her or whether he ever knew the reason. Then they released her; she was led to her home by two regular policemen, one on each side, supporting her at the elbows. The point was that she couldn't see. They had beaten her on the face, on the breasts—everywhere. So it was beatings, that and the word "lead." He could not hear of beatings or of people being led even in absurdly unconnected contexts, as when his own mother would speak of the bridegroom's mother's being led to the canopy at a Jewish wedding, without thinking of that woman and being deathly afraid. What made it odd was that he had not witnessed the scene; his mother had described it.

Véronique asked what had happened later.

He replied, I don't know, or perhaps I have forgotten that, too.

The air outside was warm when they left the restaurant. She had with her a heavy green leather raincoat, ugly and unsuited to her dress. He asked to carry it for her; folded, it weighed uncomfortably on his left arm. She took his other arm. They walked through the gloom of the garden toward the Concorde, shining, brilliant, and noisy in the distance. It was still early; the floodlights illuminating the obelisk and the horses of Marly had not been turned off. In a moment they would reach the great square. Her pace was slower. She leaned against Ben so insistently that he felt the outline and warmth of her breast. The vision in the story he had just told, mixing with Agnès at Desfossé's flickered in his mind—was this a universal signal? He let the leather coat fall on a bench and turned toward her. Before his arms could close around her she was already clinging to his body, her lips opening his. He had not misunderstood her.

BEN TOLD ME of his affair with Véronique only after it became known to Paul. These circumstances will be related in their time. What neither Véronique nor I ever told Ben—and I believe he stuck to his decision not to suspect it—was that I too had been her lover during her first college vacation, when I stayed at her mother's house in Quevrin, and during the following school year; that I had seen and followed with my lips and tongue the stigmata left by those extraordinary, secret beatings; that I beat her myself, with the palms of my hands and then also with my belt, in winter afternoon daylight, in the glacial silence of my parents' apartment—they were spending that Christmas in Eleuthera—because, after we had made love, and I had caressed her back, which was again clear as alabaster, she begged me to do it with a vehemence that shocked me and eventually separated us, for I had never done such a thing before or since. It was, therefore, not difficult, as I read the notes in which their first night together was alluded to so often, described by Ben in frenzied fragments, to be present, to remember, and to imagine.

They drove in silence to the rue du Cherche-Midi. Her mouth was glued to him, her hands were inside his shirt, unbuttoning his trousers, tugging at his necktie. At red lights he would in turn reach for her. By the time he had stopped the car before his house, their clothes were in such disarray that he was going to abandon the car on the sidewalk, but she laughed, rebuttoned him, opened the gate, shut it behind them, and said, Let's race inside. On an idiotic impulse, he carried her over the threshold; though so tall, she weighed nothing. When they were in his room—he had picked up their clothes from the floor as they made their way to it; he did not want to leave, like Hansel, a trail for poor Gianni— and at last he saw her naked, he was astonished at how heart-wrenchingly thin she was, her white body, with no remains of suntan at all, a blond isosceles triangle in the middle, ending in large slightly pink feet. Her breasts, which had felt so heavy when they embraced, were in fact only long. She bent over him. In the spasm of pleasure that ensued he thought for a terrified moment that there were scars at the ends of her breasts—what operation could she have had?— but it was only her nipples, somewhere at the end of his field of vision, pendent, astonishingly dark for someone of her color, and large.

And the rest, those actions that Ben had used to think so repetitious? They enchanted him; he had stumbled into the vast bliss of being loved. She told him how she had longed to be entered by him, that she would not stop masturbating except when he was in her. She would cover him with her juice and forbid him to wash, steal his clothes and wear them, find one million ways to be always with him.

So there we will leave them, in my cousin Olivia's bed, the French windows open on the little garden and pensive Pomona. They will sleep until the sun is quite high. Then Gianni will bring their breakfast; Véronique will sing in the bath; they will speed across Paris to get rid of the awful raincoat and pack a tiny suitcase of her clothes—just enough for the long weekend she will spend with Ben in his house.

I envied them, especially Ben, when I read about those days in Ben's documents. Véronique was so amiable—he was not accustomed to that—and Paul, or someone before or since Paul had met her, had taught her, as Ben put it, using Valmont's phrase, to do of her own will and enthusiastically the things men hesitate to ask of the most hardened whores. Or perhaps it was just the product of wide reading, the new availability of certain kinds of films, and that good nature I have just alluded to.

Notaben (unnumbered and undated):

Sunday. Again exceptionally hot. Drove to Arpajon to lunch with V and P. Laurent there for a moment, long enough to receive the London bus and Cadbury chocolate truck I bought at l'Oiseau du Paradis. Little boys so easy; pleased with any little car. Lord be praised, the world's supply of Dinky toys is inexhaustible. How different from presents for the twins—I could never make up my mind which doll I wanted. P's maman, a hardened number, also present. Could sell real estate, but doesn't, and if she did, neither she nor son would admit it. Insisted on talking to me in English—although P and V used frogspeak, then seemed reassured because I know her cousin, the rue de l'Élysée *notaire* with a collection of Caillebotte. Having that connection at last entitled me to be addressed in French. It turns out she would have liked to have P enter the cousin's *étude*—pity not to take advantage of such an opportunity, don't I

agree? Of course I agree, but if P had listened to
Maman he might have married Josette or whatever
the name of Maître Dutruc's daughter is, for that is
the only sure way to inherit a *notaire*'s practice, and
then P would not have married V, and where would
that have left me? In a state of wretched unadultery.
Let us praise what is. I do not reveal these thoughts
to Mme Decaze.

V enchanting in white cotton. Very wrinkled, could
be in *Vogue*. She has again forgotten her underwear.
Presses my foot under the table. Result: Instant
erection and greatly increased volubility. Is the latter
the reflexive product of the former or of my
panicked-prudent efforts to confuse and distract?

Meal and coffee over. Maman wishes to depart, in
the direction of Montargis—a mere fifteen
kilometers—but I am silent as a stone; after all she is
P's, not mine, and it is he who finally packs her into
his grotesque black Citroën and zooms off spitting
angry crunching gravel. We go with Laurent for a
walk through the garden and into the Montorgueils'
park. They have a pond. I teach Laurent how to skip
stones—apparently P hasn't—and the kid is in
seventh heaven, although I am no good at it.

Just as I manage to get one to bounce three times,
P reappears. Must have left Maman at the bus stop or
traveled at the speed of light. He makes a remark
about hurrying back though without much hope of
catching me before I have said good-bye and delivers
it with such bad grace that I regret having sent that

brute a bond issue to work on last week and decide to put him on a strict diet for a while. Let him learn not to bark at the hand that feeds him. V takes it much harder. She asks him for a light, and when he passes her his gold Dupont lighter (but maybe it's a fake) she throws it right into the middle of the pond, only it doesn't bounce on the way. P disappoints me further: he yells. I take my leave.

Apparently, P is not too happy about my visits to his country establishment; he prefers to lunch with me at the Automobile Club if he invites (food deplorable but cheap), and anyway he charges it to his office, or wherever I generously choose to take him. It's fear of pollution. Getting profitable work from me is OK. Having an American who isn't quite what he seems as a guest in his rural abode is, as they say here, another pair of sleeves. He doesn't know about the cleansing effect on me of America, a Harvard education, impeccable business position, and friendship with patrician Cousin Jack. And it was P, the hypocritical swine, who thought up that strange way of inviting me to their party: he hoped I would get the hint and decline! Serves him right I didn't. As he gets to know Jews better, he will realize how remarkably insensitive they can be.

V imparted this to me and by assays of bias (pun intended) I got Guy to confirm it. I must be careful with Guy. That long nose is equipped with a sense of smell. He purred when I told him I was invited to the Decazes *en famille*.

In July, Véronique and Laurent moved to Arpajon while Paul remained in Paris, but unless he worked really late or had early morning appointments, one could not be sure that he would not jump into his car and rush to the country to spend the night with his wife and son. It was such a short drive: hardly forty-five minutes if one left Paris after the rush hour. It was essential that Paul find it highly inconvenient—impossible—to return to Arpajon unexpectedly. Ben saw to it. New work for Ben's bank rained on Paul's law office; each assignment required Paul's personal attention. The early 1970s were a fairly civilized period for lawyers and bankers: summers were generally quiet; one could afford to slow down. Important men who had the ultimate power over deals were away on long vacation at their Côte d'Azur villas or on their yachts, but Ben thought up deals that he was sure those men could not resist. Each such deal had a structure of exquisite legal complexity. He explained to Paul and his own New York partners (lest they shudder at the size of legal fees paid in Paris) that the solution of such problems could not be left for the last minute; he wanted to be ahead of the competition. Therefore, he needed an inventory of financial products perfected and ready to be offered at the first available opportunity. He knew that the deadlines he set imposed a personal hardship on Paul, he would assure him, but the result would make him indispensable to the bank and establish his reputation in international financial circles in Europe and the United States. In fact, for certain of these projects he asked Paul to go quickly to New York, to lay out for the bank's American lawyers and tax advisers on the spot how obstacles previously thought insurmountable could, in fact,

be overcome by Paul's and Ben's combined wiles and imagination.

Now that Ben knew the road to the Decazes' house by
heart, he found that the forty-five minutes ordinarily needed
to reach Véronique could be cut down to thirty. He felt light:
he was in love, and he exulted in the certainty that Véronique
loved him. How could he doubt it? She telephoned him the
moment she had spoken with Paul and confirmed that once
more he was spending the night in Paris; she was putting
Laurent to bed. Ben would dine hastily and early—Gianni
radiating grave approval of his employer's new habits—shed
his office clothes, bathe, and, with the roof of his car open,
the France Musique concert turned up to full volume, concentrate his attention on beating his most recent record for speed.
So that the dog wouldn't bark, she waited outside the gate
of the property—once, on a very warm night, she appeared
from behind a stand of flowering laurel entirely naked, her
hair loose, arms opened to welcome him. The house was
dark, except for her window and sometimes the window of
the cook, Madame Julie, on the far side of the kitchen. Joos,
the Dutch au pair, went to sleep almost as early as Laurent.
Ben waited until Véronique reappeared at the window, got
the ladder she hid for his use behind the roses, climbed as far
as it reached, and pulled himself up the rest of the way
into her room. She liked to prepare refined collations: cold
chicken, cherries, and strawberries and, later in the summer,
figs, champagne. They slept very little; in the first uneven
light of dawn he would be driving back toward Paris, this
time slowly, letting the huge trucks carrying produce to the
market at Rungis roar by him as he replayed in his mind the

wonders of the night. His hands, his whole body, he thought, had the smell of Véronique. He lingered over his coffee and newspapers, putting off the moment of the bath as long as possible, when that smell would yield to Guerlain's geranium.

There were other evenings when Véronique would decide that Laurent had run around so hard that he was certain to sleep through the night without asking for her. She would call to say she was coming to meet Ben in Paris. Paul's and Véronique's apartment was on the other side of Paris, on the rue de la Pompe; Paul's office was near the Trocadéro; he had no Left Bank habits; there was no risk of running into him. Usually, Ben and Véronique had dinner at Ben's—Gianni would put it on the table and sideboard and leave them. Other times, they made love first and then went out to eat late, at the Lipp or, when Lipp closed for vacation, at the Coupole. This was not wise, but he had Véronique on his arm, he saw her face near his in the mirror across from their banquette, and they could return to the rue du Cherche-Midi as though they were going home. Several times they saw people she knew. She said it didn't matter. It was so unremarkable to be in one of those restaurants on a summer night that if one offered no explanation no one would think an explanation had been called for.

In the middle of August, Paul rebelled. He told Ben he absolutely needed a rest; so did Véronique and the child, Arpajon being unbearably hot. They were all going for two weeks to his mother's and stepfather's house in Saint-Jean-de-Luz, where his boat would be. The legal work for the bank would be covered by his partners who had already taken vacations and, if necessary, they could reach him by phone.

Ben made the customary remarks about the French idée fixe that holidays had to be taken in August, when in fact that was the best time to be in Paris, but he did not attempt to assert the authority of a client. The thought crossed his mind that he might himself spend ten days of that period in Biarritz, among valetudinarian Levantines eating their *carottes râpées* and melon in the monumental dining room of the Palais, its windows open to the view of palm-tree tops and to the Atlantic breeze—a mere fifteen kilometers away from Véronique. What things might not be accomplished in the stillness of the afternoon while Laurent took his nap and Paul was at the helm of his ship? He let the image fade. It was insanely dangerous. Already Madame Julie had made, in Paul's hearing, an unfortunate remark about how Madame startled her when she heard someone in the kitchen, and, instead of the au pair or Laurent, she found Madame herself dressed in a man's clothes—she had never seen Monsieur wear that beautiful silk shirt. Ben was convinced that Madame Decaze *mère* had eyes in the back of her head. (Madame Julie's nocturnal vision was the consequence of one of Véronique's frequent decisions to raid the fridge—she could not easily keep ice cream in her room, she complained—and of her habit of wearing Ben's clothes on these occasions.) Paul had inquired several times about this remarkable shirt or sweater, and Madame Julie, stubbornly accurate, contradicted Véronique's assertion that it was her usual black T-shirt.

So Ben traveled instead in the opposite direction, to stay with Guy Renard in Porquerolles and exorcise the ghosts of Rachel and the twins. Odile de Montorgueil was there; she was archly surprised that he had not followed Paul and Véronique to Paul's mother's house; everybody was thrilled they had become such close friends. Ben decided he disliked her. He managed to rent a *pointu*, just like the one he had used during that distant summer. Guy and he took it out to the rocks beyond the Mas du Langoustier to gather sea urchins, which tourists and day-trippers were depleting from more accessible locations. They dove until they filled three water buckets made of especially ugly pink plastic with their catch, itself chosen on the basis of a strange palette of colors—deep green or violet shading into ecclesiastic red—which indicated that these ancient bivalves were full, and then paused to warm themselves in the sun and drink the harsh local red wine out of the bottle Guy had put in the boat. When their conversation turned to dinner—that night it was to be with friends of Odile's—Guy mentioned her catty remark about Véronique and said that being alone in the boat gave him the opportunity he had looked for to offer Ben his admiring congratulations: it was worth taking on a lot of trouble for *la petite Decaze*.

Notaben 316 (dated 7/7/70):

Lunched with Paul at the Ritz today to go over the summer's work and his bills. Both impressive. I think if the All Knowing was paying attention He must have found me OK too. I didn't lay it on too thick about how ingeniously he and his *fiscaliste* had solved the tax problems and figured out the redemption of shares—no *captatio benevolentiae*—just made it clear I had read and understood all that heavy stuff. The money part was trickier, because *he* has laid it on pretty thick—30 or 50% above the normal rate? He must know I realized it. Did he think I wouldn't protest because he is indispensable (nonsense!), because I value his friendship so much (opportunity to peek at how solid French bourgeois society lives at home), or because I want to keep on flirting with Véronique? Or is he accustomed to overcharging and then bargaining over fees? A combination of the above?

Given these doubts, I could not overpay. Told him we would not challenge this set of bills—every law firm needs cash after the summer drought—but expected reductions in bills to come until a proper average rate was achieved, and I would give precise instructions to that effect. He seemed content; anyway, invited me to dinner at home, in Paris.

When I lived with Rachel, I was jealous of all the men—her late husband included—who had possessed her before I appeared on the scene (many of them I am sure I have never identified) and all those who I thought possessed her subsequently. I am not at all jealous of Paul or the other men V has dropped hints about. (I am so grateful not to be jealous that I have not tried to obtain an inventory.) Of course it's nonsense to use the verb "possess" unless I was jealous only of men whom Rachel *loved*—and even then, what kind of possession is it? But I wasn't: I was equally jealous of men who just fondled or entered her casually, transactions in which love had no part.

I don't think I am free of jealousy about Paul because V has told me that Paul wants her only rarely—what does that matter? When he does want her and takes her they surely do everything V and I do and more. (Miraculously, I have not asked myself exactly what they do, given V's ingenuity, if it is true that Paul is difficult to arouse and please.) Nor is it because she says she doesn't "love" him and they are just friends and partners. I think my paradoxically happy situation is due exclusively to V's having made me believe that she loves me and wishes me well. This appears to take away the sting of all her other activities, past and present. And I think this absence of jealousy also obtains because I love her *better* than I loved Rachel (how could I say I love her *more*), in that I trust her completely and all my feelings toward her are kind.

The discussion with Paul about money successfully concluded (from my point of view), I began to concentrate on my fruit tart—he has a sweet tooth, so I ordered dessert to keep him company—and to wonder once again what has caused V to prefer me to him. It can't be looks. Paul has a nice, open face, even teeth unstained by tobacco, although he smokes, and the sort of body that goes with tennis, soccer, and sailing. Robust and big boned. Perhaps he should keep away from sweets, though, or get Arnys or whoever else makes his shirts to cut them wider. Right now they have an unfortunate tendency to stretch across his chest and pop open at the buttons,

revealing light brown hair. There is also the problem
of his crotch. It may be that his tailor is skimping on
fabric and should be told to give more scope to Paul's
noble parts. As it is, the crotch of his trousers has
ugly wrinkles. One can't be careful enough with
women. Could these defects have repelled V? His
hands are terrific: large, with strong fingers ending in
broad fingernails shaped like shovels, sufficiently
neglected to make one remember that this is a man
who knows how to pull on a halyard, tie knots in
freezing weather, etc. The rest? He talks well,
especially in French, with a lawyer's verbosity and
self-assurance. Has read all of Sir Walter Scott in the
original—not much for us to discuss there, I have
only read *Ivanhoe* and don't remember the plot—and
likes conspiracy theories. It's amazing to hear him
prove how the CIA killed Jack Kennedy.

Then why me and not him? I don't set much store
by V's reports of sexual inadequacy—Rachel didn't
think I was such hot stuff either—and at least Paul
gave her sturdy, beautiful Laurent. I have been careful
to inform her that I cannot father a child.

Her love is a gift of the gods.

Notaben 401, dated "begun 22/ix/70" (excerpt):

V spends last night at rue du C-M. Paul in London,
where I caused him to be sent. He telephones late
and gets Joos. She gives him my home number, as V
has told her I am giving a dinner—and so I was, for

her and me, so technically speaking V was not lying. Around three-thirty in the morning, he calls again, once more waking the unfortunate Joos. No Monsieur, Madame *toujours pas rentrée*. Thereupon, the telephone rings beside my bed, but I am not out, I am not asleep, I am inside Madame. She asks me to answer; what if something has happened to Laurent. P demands furiously to know whether V is with me. I feign confusion due to deep slumber, eventually ask him if he realizes what time it is and offer to call the police or go over to his apartment and make sure everything is OK. He hangs up on me. Bad sign.

I urge V to go home at once, as he is certain to try their apartment again, but she says it makes no difference. It is already so obviously past the hour at which she would have been in her own bed if she had returned directly after my dinner that it is necessary to tell Paul the truth or another lie—no matter what, that she has gone to an all-night laugh movie—and let him storm as much as he wants. Perhaps he will beat her; that may reanimate their sex life.

A horrible, shameful surge of desire—and for the first time something like jealousy—comes over me. I reach for her. We make love again, intently. I think she knew the effect her words would have. Then we talk. She asks why, if I really love her, I don't want her to tell the truth. My house is large enough for her and Laurent; they can move in the next day; Laurent likes food just as much as she; what a nice change Gianni's cooking will be from what he gets in

Arpajon or at rue de la Pompe. She adds, We would be like this every night.

I ask if she has really thought about the consequences—scenes with Paul and in the family, how Laurent will take it, the custody fight and its unpredictable result (French courts might favor the father in this sort of case where the mother is "at fault" and I am not French), and the general upheaval in her life, as I am not going to stay in Paris forever. She is drinking the rest of the champagne Gianni put on the night table, then crosses the room to get a *langue-de-chat* to dip in it. She puts it in my mouth. Seeing her naked, paper thin and soft, although she strides like Diana the Huntress, her strangely long breasts swaying (I sometimes think of certain photographs in *National Geographic*), breasts she is so proud of and that I kiss and comfort and praise like wounded children, brings tears to my eyes. She says she will be happy with me and will make me happy too. That will make it all right for Laurent. (She has made it clear she doesn't think Paul is a "good father," but I set as little store by that as by her assessment of his sexual performance; anyway, what does it matter? If I marry V it won't be to provide Laurent with a superior home life.) Then she says, The twins have left such a void in your life. You need to have a child you can love. Laurent and you will go to the Luxembourg to the Carrousel, and you will teach him to sail his boat on the basin. His father has never done that.

But that's precisely the problem. . . .

I was finally able to prevail on V to avoid precipitous actions. For one thing, she must first talk to a lawyer. I really don't want her to lose Laurent.

The rest of Ben's note is about Paul's rage upon his return from London—he did hit Véronique, but there was no apparent erotic intention in the punch that left her with a black eye, wearing dark glasses for two weeks, and broke a Louis XVI chair from his family—his refusal to accept the cockamamy explanation for Véronique's absence, the growth of his suspicion that she and Ben were lovers, and threats by Paul to "punish" Ben if it turned out that he was right.

A UNESCO conference on advances in hybrids resistant to drought and pests, which held out hope for parts of Africa, was scheduled to take place in Paris in mid-October. This was a subject that interested me and that I knew something about, because of research I had done on my Maine precolonial Indians. The magazine agreed to my attendance and commissioned an article. The expense allowance was not generous; in any event I preferred to be with Ben. When I called to propose a one-week visit, I detected a note of initial hesitation in his voice, which he quickly blamed on uncertainty about his own travel plans and then drowned in the generous enthusiasm of his usual response to each request I made of him. I arrived on a Saturday evening, wishing to have a day free for wandering through Paris—with Ben if possible—and for relaxation before the conference opened. In my experience, such gatherings, however high their intrinsic value, induce sleep unless one is thoroughly rested or suf-

fering from a toothache. To my surprise, Ben met me at
the airport. As we sped toward the city I made a comment
about his driving; it did not seem to make him nervous, as
in the past.

Oh, he replied jauntily, that has stopped being a problem.
I have been driving a lot, and quite happily. I have things to
tell you about it.

When we got to the rue du Cherche-Midi, I noticed a
corresponding greater gaiety in the surroundings; it seemed
that Ben had really settled in. There was a profusion of cut
flowers, and plants of various sizes and shapes had been
added to the stiff—desolate, Prudence had said—ficus and
rubber trees Olivia had left to stand lonely guard before the
French windows of the drawing room. With champagne,
Gianni served canapés he must have prepared himself, instead
of the salted nuts and Dutch cheese crackers of the previous
year. Fires were blazing in both fireplaces. I regretted that
Prudence had not been able to come with me. She would
have liked the change in the atmosphere and the change in
Ben's own mood. As though he had read my thoughts, he
said he was very sorry she wasn't there and asked me to do
whatever I needed to get ready to go out. We would have
oysters and more champagne; he couldn't see how I would
have a night's sleep otherwise.

By this time, it was quite late. Ben set a fast pace. Until
we got to Saint-Germain-des-Prés, the streets were dark and
empty. Our heels made a resonating noise against the sidewalk of the sort I associate with black-and-white films about
France under occupation. I could see that Ben's standing in
the world of night owls was high: at the Lipp, it was the

owner himself, and not one of the nephews, who gravely shook his hand and then mine and showed us to the table without even a pro forma delay. There was Ben's usual fuss about categories and quantities of oysters.

When it subsided, and our glasses had been filled, Ben told me he was glad to be able to talk to me in person, instead of writing or telephoning. A row was in the making about Véronique; it was just as well that I hear about it from him; he wanted to tell me about her anyway now that it was no longer a secret he was obliged to keep, and, as I was staying with him, I would probably run into her and figure out the situation even if no one in her French family chose to mention it to me or to my mother. In the hours that followed—we were the last clients to leave the restaurant and then used all the logs Gianni had left, keeping the fire going until, dead with fatigue, we decided we had to call it a night—Ben told me much of the story I have related. The rest he confided only to his notes.

The new aspect of the situation, he said, is that Paul has become sure that it's me, and not his nerves or imagination or some unknown dark stranger. Véronique and I have been quite careless and open on the telephone, first, because I call her only when by all rights he should be at his office, and, second, because in France you can't listen on another extension to what is being said unless you get special equipment— and maybe even an authorization for it from the post office. If the telephone rings and someone picks it up, the other extensions essentially go dead. What we had not supposed was possible, but that pork did it, was that he would put a bug on his own line and make a tape that, although it is not particularly rich in intimate detail, nonetheless leaves no doubt that we see each other behind his back. Véronique has heard the tape. He likes to play it to her. I have not yet had the pleasure. But that's not the end of your cousin Paul's telephone activities. He has taken to calling me at home in the middle of the night to inform me that he has just "screwed" or is about to "screw" Véronique—the verb is his as he now speaks to me in English, probably a form of ostracism so far as he is concerned—and he also calls at the office. The calls at the office are usually threats. For instance, he has suggested that he might send the tape to the head partner of my bank— as though poor old Dwight would care who is "screwing" Madame Decaze—and has even offered to shoot me if he catches us together.

To lighten the mood, Ben continued, I once asked him why he needs to catch me with her if all he wants to do is kill me, but I don't completely dismiss this idea of his, having seen him bang away with his gun at clay pigeons, and he is so unbalanced that when I last let him into my office he was literally frothing at the mouth, making it difficult for him to speak. He also plans to notify your mother, because he holds you personally responsible for having introduced a "leper" into his domicile. Strangest of all, he hasn't made any move to stop working for me as a lawyer. In fact, some of his calls are about how we are not giving enough business to his firm. He says no real man would make the personal situation between us a pretext for injuring him financially. I have not, as it happens, given instructions to use him less. On the contrary, I continue to like sending him out of town!

I asked whether he and Véronique were still seeing each other.

Of course, Ben replied, in the afternoons, at my house. I would say every afternoon, unless something happens that makes it quite impossible for me to leave the office. In those cases, she comes in the morning, right after Joos has taken Laurent to nursery school, and I simply get to the office on the late side. This week, Paul will have to spend two nights in Brussels. That means the three of us can dine together, unless you utterly disapprove. In any case, she will come home with me after dinner. And she is coming to lunch tomorrow. She has told Paul she has to see her mother about money.

I said that it could be that I was tired, but I couldn't understand. If they loved each other and she was willing to leave Paul, why was she still living with Paul? Couldn't their lawyer—I assumed they had one—arrange some sort of separation so that she could move in with Ben or into an apartment of her own? It seemed to me that was the way these things were arranged in New York.

He doesn't want her to leave, Ben replied, he wants to keep her at any price, he wants her to love him again as in the past, and he says she will never get Laurent if she walks out. But that's only a part of the story; it's really because of me. She does love me, and I love her, and she does make me happy. Still, I have not said pack your bags or leave your clothes there, as you prefer, and come to live with me. And the reason I don't do it is Laurent. I don't want to be responsible for her losing him or having to accept some unworkable arrangement, like not being able to take him out of the country. That is the understandable and respectable reason for the situation. I keep warning Véronique that if she doesn't keep Laurent things will eventually sour between us. I am convinced that is so. It should be possible, though, for her to get Laurent on some reasonable basis if we are careful and persistent. But the secret, guilty reason is that I am afraid to have Véronique come to me with Laurent. I am out of the stepfather business; the twins put me out of it. Even if some love were left over inside me from the twins that I could give to Laurent, I would always be checking on him out of the corner of my eye, wondering whether he was throwing it away, as Sarah and Rebecca had.

There was nothing I could think of to say. We sat for a while, looking at each other, until Ben got up and opened one set of the French windows. Cold, mildewy air poured in.

I sound terrible, he told me. Like some sort of machine for grinding out words.

For some time I had felt an enormous ache encircling my skull, pressing against my eyes. It was not just Ben's revelations, however much they depressed me. I had drunk too much, and although I had taken a bath and poured into it violet crystals from an expensive-looking bottle, my skin smelled of the airplane.

Let's see what's in the icebox, I suggested.

We found sausage and Gruyère. There was bread on the counter, wrapped in a dish towel. Ben opened a bottle of red wine. We sat down and ate, hacking away at the sausage with an old, dented carving knife. I saw that Ben was weeping. The kitchen window gave on the front courtyard, toward the east.

A sort of sallow morning had begun. Ben turned off the lights in the kitchen and the drawing room and we went to bed.

I fell asleep almost at once. When I awoke, Ben was knocking on my door. He asked if I wanted breakfast before lunch, which would be served as soon as Véronique arrived. If I did, Gianni would bring it immediately. I got ready, somehow holding my headache under control with orange juice, aspirin, and Ben's bath crystals. When I went into the drawing room, Ben was still alone, standing before an open window. He was quite dressed up, considering it was Sunday and he was expecting only his mistress and his old best friend, who was the woman's cousin. I admired his tweed suit of an undefinable soft color, the beautifully matching shirt and necktie, the polish of his shoes. Cousin Olivia's ceilings were very high; perhaps because of that, or because of that sort of distance from people and objects that a hangover induces, I also found Ben very small and lonely looking. He heard my steps and turned around with a smile.

The last part of our conversation was very morbid, he said. I have those feelings of denial and despair, but they are not all that important. Just a way of conjuring bad luck: never admit you are happy! Someday, I will get around to patenting this method.

The doorbell didn't ring. Véronique must have had a key. She came into the room with her coat still on, an enormous bunch of red chrysanthemums in her arms.

Look how beautiful they are, she said. They smell like a well-kept cemetery. And I have a new street guide for Jack, Ben's is in tatters, and a necktie for Jack so he can dress up, and a sweater for Ben, so he can take his necktie off.

It was a cashmere turtleneck the color of her flowers. Ben said he would put it on at once. I saw that he was very moved. Then, at the table, while she served the food Gianni had set out, she exclaimed over how well Ben looked in his sweater, admired the wine, talked about my mother and Vassar and Ben's important work—there was a huge project, which I too had heard about from Ben, that he was looking after in Brazil—I saw that she was leaving very little to chance. She was like a maddeningly pretty nurse whose light, quick hands bandage a large wound so tenderly that the sick man thinks only how fresh looking she is and how kind and does not even notice that she has taken away the hurt. Ben did seem happier than I had ever seen him. They offered to come with me on my walk, but I vigorously refused, knowing why she was there. As I headed toward the Seine, I prayed that this was one train Ben would manage not to miss.

V

Paris, 10/xi

My lovely Ben,

 You should have let me come to Brazil with you. It would not have been nearly so bad as the mess I have made here, trying to be prudent. And you should not have urged me to go with Paul to his uncle Rémi's for the All Hallows' Eve weekend. But I listened to you, my darling, and anyway Paul was making such a fuss about Rémi and his party, saying how I was the legend of the family, how everybody was talking about me, buzz buzz, and how the only way to fix it was for us to make an appearance and be correct. So we went, and Laurent was angelic all three days, but that is not what Paul had in mind when he lectured me about good behavior.

 Rémi's château is really quite nice. By some miracle, it was not restored in the 19th century. It has an ornamental moat Rémi is especially proud of. Inside, it's dull: dark wallpaper turned brown, Second Empire furniture, some of which may be valuable, and wherever you look—antlers! He has them in every size and in every location: over doors and fireplaces, in double rows on the dining room walls, even in the bathrooms. Each one has a little copper plate that gives the date of the meet and the place where the kill occurred.

The whole horrible family was gathered—all of them monsters except for Rémi, whom I like even though he organized this witches' Sabbath, and my wonderful Lavinia. But, of course, Lavinia wasn't there. Intelligent as ever, she got away to Deauville. How could I ever have married Paul? Why didn't I break our engagement after I had met them?

On Saturday, like every week in the season, there was the meet. Uncle Rémi's hunt mostly goes after roe deer, which is a splendid thing, my adored Ben, because those animals are beautiful and clever like you and equally difficult to catch. Since he is the master of hounds, we started from his house, within the moat, right in front of the perron. The sun came out and it all looked very grand: shiny horns; hounds; members of the hunt in bottle-green coats, everybody else in black; many children, one or two as little as Laurent, on their ponies. Rémi remembered that I ride, and he had a nice gray mare for me, with good gaits and very eager.

Paul is ridiculous on horseback, but he decided he wanted to follow the hunt; in fact he had made a big point of it the day before, so Rémi's *régisseur* got a horse for him out of a rental stable, a huge bay

animal that wheezed terribly. It must have a heart
condition. This made Paul feel slighted—a very
stupid reaction: a better horse might have thrown him
(and my troubles would be over!). But he was
unhappy anyway from the start, because he was
wearing a tweed jacket while all the other men were
in hunting coats or in black.

Finally, after a lot of blowing of horns and
consultations among Rémi and the huntsmen (they
are the employees of the hunt who look after the
dogs, and they are the only people who really know
where the scent of the deer can be picked up and
what the deer will do once he is started), we set off. I
don't suppose you have seen one of these provincial
hunts. It's not at all grand and exciting like an
English print. No great open fields; no jumping over
stone fences or down muddy cliffs into rushing
streams. Just hard riding and trying to outsmart the
animal. All the villagers turn out to watch, in cars, on
bicycles, and sometimes it is they who tell the
huntsmen which way the deer has gone.

Rémi tried to match Paul up with one of the young
cousins, but he refused and told me that he expected
me to stay with him, and so I did for almost one
hour, although the wheezing of his horse was driving
me mad and got steadily worse. Also Paul was
pulling at the poor beast's mouth, which is something
one doesn't do. Then there was a moment of great
confusion. The deer must have lain down in a hollow

under a pile of leaves, they are perfect camouflage, and Rémi and the huntsmen and the rest of us just ran over him. This happens only rarely and proves one is chasing a superior animal. In any case, the dogs lost the scent completely.

At last they got it straightened out, the deer broke, and I went after him fast, catching up to Rémi, although I saw that Paul had made his horse so furious that the poor animal was just standing athwart the road, throwing his head, blocking other people, and refusing to move. Rémi and I had a lovely run through the forest and a big clearing and again in the forest, and I forgot about everything except you, my angel, until the *curée* was over (Rémi made them give me a hoof because I had done well and was a guest), and we were drinking in a village restaurant nearby. At once, everybody was asking where Paul was and I had absolutely no idea. He finally showed up, just as people were going home. He had gotten lost. You can imagine his mood, especially as the night air was turning cold and he was so charley-horsed he could hardly walk.

In Rémi's car on the way home, Paul didn't say a word to either of us. His teeth were chattering so I put a blanket over him. Then when we were in our room—I just had time to make sure Laurent and Joos were all right—he told me to pull off his boots and then he let down his britches and showed me his rear end. It had great bloody sores on it from the saddle, and the underpants were sticking to it! One would

have thought my maman had worked him over. I
burst out laughing; I couldn't help it, although I was
sorry he had hurt himself, and then he hit me twice,
on the face. It's becoming a habit.

I got away somehow and waited until he had left
to dress for dinner. The whole gang was there when I
came down, glaring because I was late, a roomful of
Decazes with just two or three of Rémi's Poitou
neighbors who fit right in with the family. They were
short one man, so Rémi put me, I can't imagine why,
next to Paul's mother. I detest that woman. She didn't
smile when I sat down and did not open her mouth
to greet me. Across from her was her cousin, Maître
Dutruc, whom I also detest. You can't have forgotten
the black warts on his nose. I introduced you to him
at our dinner in June. He is a racist. During the war
in Algeria his platoon tortured prisoners and he likes
to brag about it. On my right was some local cousin
who ate sauce with his knife and did not speak to
anybody, so that I could see he had nothing against
me personally. At the other end of the table was Paul,
making eyes at Dutruc's daughter—the younger one,
not the one he used to sleep with before we were
married. Apropos of people who don't speak, Paul did
not say a word to me either, not a single word of
apology while we were standing around drinking
whiskey—I shouldn't say "we" as the Decaze females
weren't doing any such thing. If they drink anything
at all, it's port.

I was tired from the ride and unhappy and my face

hurt from the slaps he had given me, so I drank my
wine as quickly as I could and once even gestured for
the maître d'hôtel to fill my glass. That was the first
time Mamie Decaze spoke. She hissed that I was
being indiscreet. The second time it was to call me a
tart, but that came a little later. In the meantime, all
around me they were talking about their money and
who sleeps with whom, and how much they spend on
wherever it is they shoot birds, and I even heard Paul
say he was going to sell the house in Arpajon and get
something smaller in Sologne to be close to good
shooting—which he had never discussed with me and
after all it's my house and I was thinking of you and
how, if I were in Brazil, you would kiss me and touch
me until I was weak with pleasure. So, on an
impulse, without knowing in advance what I would
do, I stood up, tapped my knife against the wineglass,
and said, Up yours, *la famille Decaze*, I won't be in
your way much longer, because I am leaving Paul to
live with my beautiful, clever, funny Ben. And then I
told them all about you. They were so stunned that I
managed to make quite a speech.

I won't try to describe the *bordel* that followed, but
please don't feel sorry for me. I don't care what they
say or what they do. I want to be with you. Take me,
Ben, take me now.

I have asked your secretary, who is adorably kind,
to make sure this letter reaches you quickly.

Your
Véronique

But Ben was not in Brazil; he had left unexpectedly for Tokyo, where he stayed for more than a week. As they had decided to avoid the telephone, news of this change of plans had not reached Véronique. Her letter was waiting for Ben at his hotel in Rio de Janeiro.

VI

Excerpts from Notaben dated Tokyo, 29/11/70:

Sunday in Tokyo.

I stop the taxi at Toranomon Station and make my way to the Ginza. How to buy a present for V that won't compromise her?

At Takashimaya, everything tawdry or opulent prewar Mitteleuropa provincial: cream-colored embroidered tablecloths and napkins (the latter in every size), cloisonné boxes (for storage of ancestral ashes?), toothpick holders, seemingly useless bottles, figurines. In the basement, a treasure trove of Edo and Meiji prints. Bargain prices. No place for them on Olivia's walls even if I wanted to carry them to Rio and then back to Paris, which I don't.

Out.

Grinding fatigue. Thank God there is no sun. Sidewalks crowded. Schoolgirls in navy-blue uniforms. Nice round faces, pigtails, fixed smiles. Below, mostly bad legs. Also boys in matching uniforms, except they have visored caps and acne. One accosts me: Please, sir, may I speak English with you? *Non parlo inglese*, replies the brute inside me.

Leave hateful, cluttered Hibiya on my left and walk toward the hotel. Outer Palace Garden. Naked. Tortured, pampered pine trees. Crows the size of ducks overhead. Three black swans accompany me, gliding along the moat.

At once, in the hotel arcade, I find the perfect thing. A pale bud vase of such beauty that I ache to give it to V. The shopkeeper tells me it's celadon and I trust him and pay what he asks. She can say she bought it for pennies in the rue Saint-Honoré. Paul won't recognize it for what it is.

Pity that van Oppers didn't come with me. Had he been at the meetings with the city banks he would have a better idea of why he pays me to make his Brazilian dreams come true.

All week in the Bank of Tokyo conference room. Sonorous name: one expects transplanted Victorian grandeur—rather like those salons of the Algemene Nederland in Amsterdam, where portraits of burgher directors hang cheek by heavy jowl with the photograph of Prince Bernhard, when still an employee, carnation in his buttonhole, bending over a ledger—only here it should be Japanese barons in cutaway coats, like Hirohito but sturdier and ferocious. Nothing of the sort. Did the firebombings or MacArthur sweep it all away, or did the Japanese do the job themselves? I find a room like the lobby of a good-class motel, with a potted plant or two in the corner no better than the rubber plant at rue du C-M

that Véronique makes fun of. In the middle, a long
Swedish or Danish coffee table—one of those affairs
that might be made of teak but probably isn't, on
either side a row of brown armchairs (from the same
motel but with white, sparkling-clean antimacassars
on armrests and where one's head might recline).
Behind them, two long sofas covered with green
plastic matter imitating leather. Yet farther removed,
in profusion, stackable chairs with metal tube legs.
Disconsolate, East-meets-West "art" on the walls.
Fields of something or other, flowers, a mountain or
two, fishermen dragging seines toward the beach,
done in the manner of van Gogh, Renoir, and Monet,
with that admixture of eccentricity of color and angst
I have come to recognize as indigenous.

The day I arrive, the principals are lined up to
greet me, in order of rank, naming themselves and
their banks twice—at the handshake and upon the
presentation of the business card that they manage
with the dexterity of riverboat gamblers. I, too, have
cards and in both languages, but deal them out like a
rube, wasting precious seconds fiddling with the
paper clip that holds them. Beyond the receiving line,
an undifferentiated crowd mills about: bubbly, eager,
fresh-faced junior "staffs" (I have found that this
noun when used in the singular signifies individual
members of the team, while the plural denotes them
collectively; oversized walking sticks have some other
designation, as yet unknown to me), and also older,

ineffably seedy men—assistant managers and deputies outdistanced in the race for promotion, loyally, bravely awaiting retirement. Second round of card exchanges, introductions, smiles, and bows: these men are not like spear bearers in *Aida*; it is they who formulate decisions their sleek bosses will in the end approve and announce. Woe to him who neglects them.

We settle down.

I find I am alone in the middle of my row of armchairs (the Lord is my staff, may His presence fill the empty seats on my right and on my left). Facing me across the table (upon which simpering and desirable young ladies are placing bowls of green tea) is the Bank of Tokyo, all atwinkle and personified by Mr. Osamu Yoshida, the directors of the other syndicate banks placed at his sides in descending order of their participation in the loan. Yoshida, who knows English well enough to do the *Herald Tribune* crossword puzzle in ink, announces we will have interpretation—"so all members and staffs will have good understanding. Please be patient."

All right. Let time pass if in the end it will turn into money.

Gradually, I get the drift. That they want to make the loan, essentially must make it, is beyond question: the Japanese chemical companies are keen on the Brazilian product. If the construction of the project is not financed, they won't get it. MITI wants the chemical companies to have all the feedstock they need. Ergo, the banks should solve their problems. But how and at what cost they will do it is far from clear. The banks are stuck on two points, and they are related: they and the chemical companies who will borrow from the banks want Japanese government political-risk insurance, and they need a mortgage on the project because without the mortgage they may not get the insurance, or, if they get it, the premium will double.

So far so good, although it's hard to see what use the mortgage will be to the banks or the Japanese government if it has to pay for expropriations or civil war in Brazil! And the Brazilians don't mind giving the mortgage—the problem is that for reasons of "policy" the World Bank wants one too, and being the World Bank naturally it wants a first mortgage. On the other hand, neither the Japanese banks nor whoever in the Ministry of Finance pulls the insurance strings will accept being in the second place and having a second mortgage. This is a mixed question of banking prudence and national pride, where I guess considerations of pride weigh heavier.

We examined at three meetings my first solution, which I rather liked but the ministry rejected: it was to have the World Bank agree that—although its mortgage would rank first—it would hold any money it recovered in a single pot and share it equally with the Japanese banks as second mortgagees. From my point of view, a lead-pipe cinch, requiring at most a two-page letter of understanding. But it bothered the ministry to have the World Bank as a big brother or guardian for the Japanese banks, and the banks, for all the noisy sucking of air between their teeth, couldn't budge the bureaucrats. In the end, perversely, I felt relieved, because I had put forward my solution without finding out whether the Bank wished to be a big brother!

Impasse. Mr. Yoshida's assistant drones on translating my most recent remarks, which must be quite titillating, for Mr. Yoshida holds up his hand, says "Just a moment please," and they fall to chattering among themselves in Japanese with no thought of translation for my benefit. While they are so engaged, I have an illumination. What if I proposed giving the World Bank and the Japanese banks each a mortgage over the same property, each mortgage to have equal rank? True, to my knowledge no such thing has ever been done in Brazil or elsewhere, but there is always a first time; the Brazilian national motto is Order and Progress, and this is nothing if not progress. Best of all, it occurs to me that in case we can't get all the right lawyers to give the right opinions, I will surely be able to talk the World Bank into signing a sharing-of-proceeds agreement between it and the Japanese banks as though they were both first mortgagees, which will have the same effect as my first solution but won't make anybody the big brother or keeper of anybody else. Then, the lawyers' opinions will matter very little.

Taking brusque advantage of a pause in the hubbub, I advance my proposal.

Eureka! Another "Just a moment please," and I am pleased to restate what I have just said in slightly different words. This time, Yoshida doesn't even bother with "Just a moment." While they debate, I survey the audience. Notwithstanding the high drama, a good number of the "staffs" are "resting their eyes." Others are taking notes. Will they share them with the sleepers? I think so. That way everybody can file a report. Mr. Yoshida's assistant, who doesn't miss a beat, is perorating. In the excitement of the thing, he has stood up; he uses an English word or two in every sentence so I can almost follow the exegesis of my new invention.

Mr. Yoshida thanks me. Would I mind waiting just a little, while they call the ministry? I smoke a cigar and drink my fourth cup of tea. Sad not to be able to flirt with the tea lady.

Yoshida's assistant and a team of others return from wherever they used the telephone. The ministry is pleased; they will want to "check" the proposal again, but it's so very nice and clear there should be no problem.

Airline schedules. Yoshida and a mission from each other bank will be ready to go to Rio next week—this is a good sign—but, horror of horrors, they settle on the flight I am already booked on. Instantly, I lie about my departure plans. I love them all dearly, but I need to be alone. And they will like it better too.

Five in the afternoon here, nine in the morning in France. Will she be the first to pick up the receiver, will I hear the silver of her laughter? Breaking our new rule, I try Arpajon. No answer. Wave of discouragement. No reason to think Paul is not recording calls in Paris. I can't pretend I am Lavinia! I give up.

VII

THE PETROCHEMICAL PROJECT that had taken Ben to Rio de Janeiro and then, abruptly, to Tokyo when the financing to be supplied by Japanese banks seemed to founder was sponsored by a Brazilian conglomerate. A Belgian consortium advised by Ben's bank was to participate and engineer many of the facilities. The other foreign partner in the project was an American company whose name was a household word in many countries. The relations among the parties were tense. But the American negotiators were relieved to find at the side of the Belgians a partner of a New York investment bank as renowned as their own company. Ben and the government economist advising the Brazilians had been friends at Harvard, so gradually he assumed the role of everyone's father confessor. Negotiating on behalf of the Belgian group became mediation and a search for a result that would be fair to all. Ben was exuberant about what he had accomplished: the professional challenge was considerable, greater than any he had faced, and he liked its being intellectual as well as political. The peacekeeping function suited the Belgians. They told him they were pleased. There was no doubt in Ben's mind about the line he must follow to reach solutions that would work and be acclaimed by all as brilliantly inventive. Being liked and trusted by all, seeing Mr. Nagao, the head of the largest Japanese chemical company and the spokesman in this transaction for the four other companies that would also be buyers of the product (in theory waiting in the wings for the project to coalesce but in fact present at most of the big meetings), prefer his analysis of problems to that of his Japanese colleagues, so much so that after the meetings he sought out Ben to talk "heart-to-heart," as he put it, was a sweet Ben could not resist. Besides, he was relieved to be away from Paris and the need to come to a decision about Véronique. The notes I have pored over, and talks I had with him in New York early in the following year, leave no doubt that he was quite conscious of this aspect of his feelings. He said it was a great sensation, like playing hooky—Isn't that, he asked me, how all happily married husbands feel when they are away from wifey?

When he picked up Véronique's letter at the concierge's cramped desk in the annex building of the Copacabana Hotel, he read it immediately while that dignitary's assistants fussed over his luggage. It was not unlike a truant officer's summons. He read it again, in the living room of his suite. The weight of the two-day flight was like a lead cloak. Who could tell what had happened since the letter was written? He looked at his watch and calculated the hour in Paris. It was too late and too risky to telephone Véronique. A call to Madame Duhot, his discreet and sensible secretary, was the thing: he would ask her to get in touch with Véronique the next morning. He composed the number and listened for a long time to its thin and useless ring. Should he try Véronique himself before dawn in Rio, if he managed to be awake at that hour despite his fatigue? Exasperation quickly turned into sputtering, uncontrollable anger—at Paul, at Véronique, at himself, and at the circumstance itself of the letter's reaching him just at that particular moment.

The meetings with the Brazilian Ministry of Finance and the World Bank scheduled for the next day were all-important: unless they went well, the World Bank would not lend money for the electric plant needed to service the petrochemical plant or for the enlargement and dredging of the harbor. Without that cheap money, which would be Brazil's sovereign debt and not the project's, the entire undertaking would have to shrink. His success would be solid, not brilliant—another well-done job, nothing more. How could he be expected to solve the puzzle of his own feelings about living with Véronique—marrying her, no less!—to reassure her, and to give her, from six thousand miles away, counsel on how to deal with her barbarian husband, when all his attention and feelings, yes, feelings, were concentrated on what he must do tomorrow? He must find time, first thing in the morning, to review again his solution for the mortgage problem with his own lawyer and the lawyers for the other participants and wrest from them a common position of approval in principle. Of this he was confident. Then he would have to extract, in the course of one ministerial audience, from a nationalist government operating under the eyes of an agitated economic press, sufficient concessions, some of substance, some of form, some trivial, and some quite important, to convince a bevy of World Bank bureaucrats trained at Tübingen, Cambridge, and Chicago that they were at last "getting a grip" on a relevant segment of the Brazilian budget. That the ingredients to mix such a cocktail were at hand, he was completely sure. The stumbling block would be, as usual, human obtuseness and obstinacy; instead of accepting a hard-won offer on the spot, the World Bank's Dr. Fritzler would mutter something on the order of "*Ja schon gut*, maybe I consult Washington," and while "maybe" he consulted, the minister would withdraw whatever offer he had made, leave for a holiday in the mountains, dissolve into thin air.

The sun had declined in the direction of the mountain. Ben looked out the window at the huge rectangular pool, now partly shaded, and beyond, toward the bay. Between the wing of the hotel and the new apartment building facing it he could see only a slice of deep blue. It occurred to him that he could think about Véronique only a little bit at a time, like Swann's father about his beloved late wife. Possibly, he could not remain angry very long either. There were huge beach towels in the bathroom scrolled with the name of the hotel. He went down to the pool. In the area still in the sun, on deck chairs, around little tables, sat or reclined men and women with bodies the color of ancient gold, darker than the chains on their necks and wrists. Their stomachs were incredibly flat. Self-control, constant exercise, or secret successes of Brazilian plastic surgery? Gentle voices in incessant talk surrounded him—Ben thought it was like an aviary with no roof where the birds had been taught to speak Russian. That was the true sound of Carioca Portuguese. A solitary, elderly figure was doing exquisitely slow laps up and down the pool. Ben found a chair for his towel, made the diving board thump, and swam until his eyes could no longer bear the sting of the chlorine.

He did not call Véronique or Paris at dawn. Having taken a new sort of sleeping pill recently prescribed by his doctor for travel insomnia, he slept without dreaming. Then, rested but feeling somehow disconnected from his surroundings and from the task at hand, he read over his notes. The coffee tasted bitter. Once more, he confirmed his dislike for papaya. On the other hand, the guava jelly and white cheese, those staples of a Brazilian morning, began to make him feel that he might yet recover the alacrity of spirit and cheer of mind he badly needed. In *O Globo* he parsed out a description of Willy Brandt kneeling at the monument to the dead of the Warsaw ghetto, visibly overcome by emotion. A well-done background paragraph in the article discussed the recent recognition of the Oder-Neisse line, the burning of the ghetto in 1943, the ultimate destruction of Warsaw a little over a year later, and the extraordinary care with which Poles had rebuilt their capital. Always when he found himself in a strange city, Ben skimmed the pages of the telephone directory, looking for his own name and other surprises. The Rio book listed many Jewish names, extravagantly spelled. Feinbaum from Galicia had become Vainboim. Others retained special, Polish transliterations: Bernsztajn instead of the banal Bernstein; Grynszpan, Lakman, Szpigel, others. They were presumably the clever ones who had smelled a rat in '36 or '37 and hightailed it to the land of the coffee bean and moon-shaped beaches—and their happy descendants. It was nice that they too had *O Globo* to cheer them at breakfast.

He shook himself and summoned the lawyers. At eleven, they were still arguing in his living room. He was glad to leave them there. They would find it easier to see the matter his way once he was out the door.

The group was assembled by the time he came downstairs—the Japanese in greater number than he might have wished; van Oppers, the head of the Belgian consortium; and Rawlson, representing the American team and the senior of his Chicago lawyers, both grim and concentrated, breast pockets bulging with ballpoint pens and mechanical pencils. Carvalho, the manager of Rawlson's Rio subsidiary, resplendent in hand-stitched gabardine, was busy giving directions to the drivers. Ben, van Oppers, and Mr. Nagao got into the same car. Mr. Yoshida, still surprised to have arrived in Rio on a different flight than Ben's, was not sure what he should do. Ben advised him to hang back. Attending the meeting could only lead to overly hasty arrangements. He should come to the celebratory lunch, if there was to be one.

When your turn comes, don't make an opening statement, he advised Mr. Nagao, just tell the minister how honored you are to be included in the meeting. Let Fritzler and the minister do the talking, as they must if we wait long enough. They won't be able to tolerate the silence. Then, when the World Bank's flank is exposed, I will explain that the Belgian and Japanese groups are prepared to trust everybody—the Bank, Rawlson, the Brazilian side—that thanks to the cooperation of Japanese city banks, present even now in Rio though not at the meeting, the funds to build this project have been committed, the market is waiting for the product, but that the funds will remain blocked unless everyone agrees to a simple, workable scheme. This scheme I have right here, written out on one page. You will see: once the minister feels frustrated enough it won't even be necessary to convince him. The Bank will suddenly see that the meeting is almost over and it has no proposal of its own on the table. That's when they will accept ours, rather than have every journalist in Brazil write that the World Bank's representatives sabotaged the Pedra Branca project. McNamara wouldn't be amused. Let time and inertia work for us.

The meeting was over. The minister invited the Bank representatives and the other participants in the project to initial Ben's paper and then he initialed it himself. An important step has been taken on the road to Brazil's development, he declared. Ben realized that his face had turned pink with pleasure, the shade of the summer necktie he was wearing. He told me that he had wished someone who cared about who he really was had been there to see him pull it off—his mother and father were dead, but perhaps Véronique, except that she wouldn't have been able to keep herself from giggling, or for that matter myself. Instead he posed for photographs with the minister, van Oppers, Mr. Nagao, and Rawlson, first for members of Mr. Nagao's staff, each of whom seemed equipped with a camera, and then for journalists and a television crew. The suspense was over. After lunch, he would draft a press release; the next order of business, while the group was still assembled in Rio, was to pin down the text of the mortgage-sharing agreement and to settle on a schedule for the preparation and signing of contracts. This was lawyers' work. He wanted it done quickly. The thought of lawyers reminded him of Paul and therefore

Véronique and caused an unpleasant contraction in his heart.
For that was his other task for the afternoon: he must write
to Véronique.

*Undated draft of letter from Ben to Véronique (translated from
the French by me):*

My love,

    I have had your letter since yesterday; it languished
here for too many days while I was en route to
Tokyo and then back to Rio, confused by these
devilish changes in time zones, reluctant to call you
even when the hour seemed perhaps propitious,
reluctant to write. I don't trust your concierge. She is
perfectly capable of purloining mail and she may have
been incited to do so. This letter will get to you
quickly and safely. I am entrusting it to a charming
young Frenchman who leaves for Paris tomorrow and
will deliver it into the very hands of Madame Duhot.
She will telephone you and make further arrangements. When you speak to her, please say how much
her discretion and loyalty have meant to us.

    What a brave girl you are! They might have killed
and skinned you (like the poor beast you finally
cornered that afternoon) after you finished your
remarkable after-dinner speech—perhaps by now
they have, but I rather think not. Such things are
more likely done when the tribe is still gathered, an
unprogrammed but logical prolongation of the rite
being celebrated. That you were able to write to me

from Paris after the weekend inclines me to think
they resisted—perhaps never truly felt—the urge for
instant retribution and purification. On the other
hand, they are deep and calculating. Possibly, they are
still thinking it all over, deciding what to do.
"Vengeance is a dish that's best eaten cold." I can't
recall who said it, perhaps it's just a proverb, but it
might have been invented with your Decazes in mind.
I wrote these last sentences just to scare myself.

All this is by way of a lighthearted prologue. One
more misguided attempt to be funny! You know—I
cannot doubt it for a moment—I adore you, and my
happiness (you have accustomed me to think that I
am capable of being happy) has only you as the
source. Incredible though it is, you have also
accustomed me to believe that you love me. So, since
Paul is not giving up (I admire him for it), you are
free to choose what will follow. I have told you what
I am like inside—barren, dark, and desperate—and
you have had some opportunities (perhaps
insufficient) to see that it is not some grotesque form
of coquetry that leads me to speak of myself in such
terms. Also, I am not as rich as I seem. My income is
large, but I have spent my money like a man who has
no accounts to render to anyone but himself, and no
one's future to care about. Such capital as I have is
locked up in my firm and at the risk of its business.
There will be no inheritances from parents or celibate
aunts and uncles, no farms or houses in the country,

no buildings behind the Opéra slowly turning into mountains of ducats.

If we are lucky and you have custody of Laurent, he will have a stepfather to grow up with instead of a father. Will I be a good stepfather? It is certain that I like children. And, as I love you, I will probably in time become very fond of Laurent—I certainly loved the twins I always talk about when I was their stepfather. But I think that, along the way, I have lost some quality of the heart—warmth? spontaneity?— which young children need. I doubt Laurent will believe that I love him or that he will love me, and I fear the consequences. Right or wrong, my anxiety is real, and therefore you should take it into account. Whatever is to become of me, I implore you to be prudent.

I must remain here a little longer—a matter of days, I think—and then, the moment I have finished, I will hurry back, possibly via Tokyo. I suppose that by then you will, in any case, be in Verbier with Laurent. In fact, I imagine you now in the red snowsuit and helmet I have so admired in photographs, speeding past astonished mortals, the sun brilliant and high, your upturned, smiling face turning the color of honey.

Shall I add a word about the activities here? We triumphed this morning, and the minister approved everything one might have reasonably expected, and then we drank to this "white stone" project at a

lengthy, solemn lunch given at the Jockey Club.
Nothing more different from the institution at rue
Rabelais can be imagined: a pompous, modern office
building in downtown Rio, with a branch at the
racetrack near the beach at Gávea; one can even have
one's hair cut here. I was eager to leave and write
this letter, but even so I could not help being amused.
Brazilian, American, Belgian, and Japanese flags were
everywhere—tiny ones on tables, bigger versions,
like bouquets of dried flowers fastened to walls—a
legion of waiters in white gloves sticking their fingers
into the sauce, and heavy local red wine. The minister
is like a mountain, with one of those well-massaged
bodies—does he have himself worked on at this very
club?—and surprisingly tiny feet and hands, pomaded
hair parted in the middle, and the best black silk suit I
have ever seen, with the sort of cut and detail work
one has not encountered in Europe since the war. I
was on the verge of asking him for the name of his
tailor and then remembered I wouldn't be here long
enough to have even a first fitting. My Belgian pals
lapsed into absolute mutism. Contentment? Effort of
shoveling in and digesting the *feijoada completa*? I will
never know. As Rawlson couldn't understand a word
of the minister's English, I was left with the burden
of conversation. Tonight, more conversation. I
suppose I will dine with van Oppers, Nagao, and
Yoshida—and however many acolytes they choose to
bring along.

Now I will leave you to go for a swim in the
ocean. I should have said that I will *try* to swim. The
breakers look regular and friendly from a distance but
close up they are probably terrifying.

Fervently and humbly I kiss you in each particular,
in each part, lingering most you know where.

                                                        Ben

In fact, during that afternoon, possibly after he wrote,
corrected, and copied the letter, Ben decided that he would
not leave Brazil as soon as his work was done. It would have
been possible to finish the matters requiring his personal
attention in Rio by the next morning, if he had insisted, so
that he could have caught the night flight to New York, and
then, after a day spent at the office, he could have gone on
to Paris. Or he could have gone to Paris via Tokyo, as he
had written to Véronique that he might. But a profound,
paralyzing lassitude was overtaking him, a need to yawn,
stretch, and sleep. He called his friend Carvalho and asked if
there was any place on the seashore near Rio where he could,
for a few days, lie in the sun and swim. He didn't want to
stay in the city: the beach was too crowded, the water in
front of the hotel was too rough and at times possessed a
curious smell, and the pool at the Copacabana, though better
than most pools, was chlorinated, boring, and for the best
part of the afternoon shaded from the sun.

Carvalho thought the mountains would be better and
healthier and offered to take Ben to his own place in Petró-
polis, above Rio, but Ben insisted on the sea. There were two

possibilities: Cabo Frio to the north, which was newly chic and discovered by the French, but because of its vegetation would remind Ben of Montauk rather than East Hampton, or, to the south, Angra dos Reis, the domain of the middle class, where no foreigner had ever set foot. There was a small, somewhat primitive hotel Carvalho knew, accessible by car if one wanted to drive for eight hours over a winding mountain road or in less than an hour by a single-engine plane Ben could charter. The hotel had a clientele of families with children, but Carvalho thought a quiet room might be available. Ben could rent a fisherman's motorboat and go each morning to a different, remote, and completely deserted beach. The bay, Carvalho guaranteed him, was the most beautiful in the world, almost untouched by progress. If he was willing to struggle in Spanish and Portuguese to make himself understood, that was where Ben should go. Ben agreed. Angra sounded like the realization of a forgotten dream. He asked Carvalho to help him book a room and an airplane.

Then he went swimming after all. The beach, across the street from the hotel, was still full of people. At its edge, wizened dark men sold large cloth kites the shape and color of *araras*. Clutches of them strained on strings tied to posts fixed in the sand. Other men just like them, heavy metal containers hung on each side of their bodies, walked among the supine sunbathers offering a cold *mate* drink and fruit juices. Every hundred meters or so a volleyball game of what seemed professional quality was in progress. Ben walked slowly toward the water, dazzled by the light, which he saw for the first time that day without the filter of sunglasses or

tinted windows, once more marveling at the beauty of the
hoary, prehistoric shape of the Pão de Açúcar beyond the
huge rock at the end of the beach, beyond the laughter and
talk all around him. These were the poor people. He had
learned from Carvalho and others that Copacabana, now that
it could be reached by bus, was the preserve of modest shop
and office employees and workers and youngsters from the
favela. Boys and girls of the middle class were to be seen at
Ipanema and Leblon, perhaps the beaches beyond. The rich
were in the shade of beach umbrellas at the swimming pools
of the Country Club in Ipanema or the Yacht Club or perhaps
the Copacabana Hotel. Living in penthouses of certain gleaming apartment buildings on avenida Atlântica, sometimes they
ventured out for an early morning walk on the beach, their
bodies covered against the sun. Except for a natural sal-
lowness, the faces of the rich were as pale as Ben's. Although
no one looked at him—he felt that he was passing quite
unseen—he was acutely conscious of the whiteness of his
body and his floppy Brooks Brothers trunks. In France, on
the Côte d'Azur and in Porquerolles, those trunks had certainly stood out, a sign of a certain elegance among the
ambient bikinis. Here they connoted deprivation, absence of
ease; they hung on him, he thought, like the odd-shaped,
baggy clothes he had worn as a refugee. Occasionally he saw
other white bodies on the sand, lying facedown, in swimming
gear similar to his, angry red flush covering the shoulder
blades, backs of arms, the mounds of fat pushed up by the
elastic at the waist. Were they all airline stewards, he wondered, or Dutch environmentalists traveling on worldwide
passes?

The water, when he finally reached it, was studded with those enviable brown bodies standing knee-deep and splashing. Farther out, more brown bodies were streaking beachward on their surfboards. Others were paddling out in search of the perfect wave. No one was swimming. That was, he realized, because the waves were even bigger than they looked from his window or from the outer edge of the beach. But if he could judge by the color of the water, they broke where the water was already deep. He decided he would chance it; unless his head was torn off by an errant surfer, he would be all right. He swam steadily until he had passed the last surfboards. Then he turned to rest and admire the view of the bay. Seen from the water it was as glorious as he had expected, green until the beach, then white, then green again where the mountains began above, the sky blue with little round clouds. He also noticed that, instead of the waves carrying him back toward land as he had expected, a current was taking him out to the open sea. Niterói lay far to the north. That was not where he was drifting; except for tiny islands farther in the bay there was nothing he knew of between him and South Africa. He remembered being told that a long pipe spews out Copacabana sewage some distance away from the beach; treated sewage that, in any case, is harmless to bathers due to offshore currents. Was this one of those currents, how far was the end of the pipe, did sharks gather at its outlet? He began to swim toward shore, abandoning the crawl in favor of a dogged breaststroke, trying to keep, as he had been taught one must, on a line oblique to the current so as not to fight its full force. Possibly he was

making progress; at any rate, he was no longer being pushed
back. Except for the thought of sharks, which he tried to keep
out of his consciousness, he began to feel great awe and
rejoicing. What if he tired and drowned: Could it happen in
a setting that was more paradisal? A small corner of the
curtain that hides the unhoped-for life to come was being
lifted. He had always liked to leave parties on the crest of the
wave, when the dance floor was still crowded, before early
morning fatigue decomposed the faces of the hosts. This
would be just such an exit. He thought about Pedra Branca,
his office in Paris, Madame Duhot, and his apartments. Except
for Véronique, his affairs were in perfect order, and even
Véronique's problems, especially if she did not in the end
mind remaining with Paul, were bound to be eased by this
exotic accident: the messy questions about life with her could
remain without an answer. He had once told his father that
he felt a tropism toward death. The old lawyer had laughed
and replied that he had it in common with all forms of life.
Perhaps that was so; at least he acknowledged it gratefully.
This would be the ultimate extinction of his family; there
would be no more pyrotechnics staged by Ben for an audience
of one; his well-cared-for body had but a single task to perform before it was set free. He turned and began a lazy but
perfect crawl in the direction of the unknown. That was the
way; in a while he would reach the point of no return.

He did not know how much time passed before he began
to meet resistance, a force stronger than the one before, when
he was swimming for the beach. He understood that he had
drifted into another, rapid and colder current that was taking

him this time toward land, probably to the limit of the Copacabana Beach, where a small fort ended its perfect curve. Was this a sign? He would let the current and his own endurance decide. Without breaking the rhythm of the stroke, he aligned his body with the current.

He staggered out of the water just ahead of the rocks, at the very end of the beach. The afternoon had turned pigeon gray. Some boys playing soccer shouted at him. He shook his head and waved his hand at them uncomprehendingly. Then he saw the ball at his feet. He kicked it in their direction. They shouted at him again. Keeping to the edge of the water, where the sand was hardest, he began the long walk back to the hotel. Neither his shirt nor towel were at the place where he thought he had left them. Except for the volleyball players, the beach was very quiet. Ben combed his hair with his fingers, carefully brushed the crust of sand off his ankles and feet, and crossed the street. The man who handed out towels to guests was still in the doorway at the pool. Ben took one, wrapped it around his shoulders, and went into the lobby of the annex. Messages were waiting for him, from van Oppers and Rawlson about dinner arrangements. Ben asked the concierge to call and say that he was detained in town and would not return in time to join them. When he reached his room he saw his letter to Véronique and rejoiced that he had written it: it did not read like much of a love letter but it was fair; as fair as he knew how to make it. He hoped she would not be put off by his candor; he would have to take that risk. Rapidly, he scribbled a note, called the floor waiter, and asked him to put the note and the letter in the mailbox of the Frenchman leaving for Paris, and to return with tea and a double scotch.

Excerpts from a Notaben (undated and unnumbered):

Carvalho wakes me from a sleep like death. I don't know how long the telephone had been ringing. He says, Come to my place, we are having a party. The dentist I told you about is here.

Is this a dream? I look at my alarm clock: ten-thirty. Morning? Night? The curtains are drawn. Meanwhile Carvalho keeps talking, telling me he is in the company suite, two floors up, they have food, he knows I have not eaten. Now I remember the dentist: a German who settled in Rio soon after the war. Made Carvalho's front teeth. Knows everybody. In the background people are laughing over the sound of samba. My voice sounds like hell when I answer. I say I have a headache and need a bath. If I feel better, I will be up.

My face is beet red in the bathroom mirror. Reflection of the sun during all that time, I guess, even though I swam with my face in the water. I make the bath hot, because I still feel a chill, and pour in all the oils and gels I can find to fix my skin. Eventually I feel better and very hungry, so why not go to Carvalho's? One never knows what to wear in Rio: an open shirt and blue jeans or one's best dark suit. I decide on the former and soon knock on his door.

Large living room, larger than in my suite, with a giant television. Very brightly lit. I see four, maybe five, young women, girls really, young and blond, some men who must be Americans according to their girths and haircuts (judgment confirmed first by their speech and then by introductions; chemical-engineer types working for Rawlson or Carvalho), an older woman in black with unnatural anthracite hair, and Carvalho himself talking to a man who must be sixty, very sharp in a blue silk outfit. This must be the dentist. I approach and shake hands. Dr. Willi knows all about me. We get onto New York café society, and again he knows everyone. There isn't a single old biddy whose bridgework he hasn't fixed. Hauls out a pale lizard wallet to show me the X ray of Mary Lasker's jaw! I laugh and ask if he is in love with her. Quick as a wink, he tells me he is no Hans Castorp, ha! ha! ha! So nice we both like high literature, not true? Wants to look at my teeth and gums. I almost bite his hand, but not before he observes the inflammation of the lower right quadrant. I don't know how this gets us on the subject of the war, but as I eat my cold roast beef he tells me he was with the Wehrmacht on the eastern front and was lucky to be taken prisoner by the Americans near Salzburg, after the retreat. Then got to Brazil via Trieste. I inform him of my presence on the same front, in a manner of speaking, and we examine that subject and its effect on the formation of our respective characters dispassionately—as he puts it, like men of the world.

Carvalho has left us. Probably bored by ancient history. I ask Dr. Willi who are the bimbos and the *dame des toilettes*. Even as we converse, my consciousness of the minuteness of their dresses in relation to their busts, posteriors, and thighs has been growing, unchecked. Ah, he says, they are my little protégées, he says, good German girls from the state of Rio Grande in the south, near Pôrto Alegre. He goes on to explain that there are whole towns where nothing but the language of the Führer is spoken, so that's where he finds them, that's how he is able to introduce them to his special patients and friends.

Scales fall from my eyes. It's the stars. In my life, sex and dentistry are to be inextricably allied.

There is one I know will be just right for you, the Doctor continues. Allow me.

A gesture and she stands before me, smiling. A picture postcard from Tyrol, curly haired and blue eyed. Her name is Lotte. The old pander is right. I like her. How long is it since I left Paris? I think I will faint if I touch the skin on her arm. The details of her costume sink in: her particular miniskirt is flared—rayon, green leaves and yellow flowers on a background of white; she is wearing a poor little girl's white sweater, washed many times over and very clean. It buttons down the front. Herr Doktor points to a love seat. Sit down, he says, and get acquainted.

We do as told and right away she curls up so that her knees are pressed against my legs. I watch the blond, almost white, baby down on her thighs, knees, and calves. Before I realize what I am doing, I stroke her thigh. Since in the act I lean over her, she opens

her mouth for me to kiss. It is very wet. She has a
large, unhurried tongue. If I come, she will see the
stain spread, and I almost want her to; it will be my
homage. Instead, although my heart is pounding, I
recover enough to break the kiss and try
conversation. She laughs at my kitchen Spanish.
German works better; the sort of things I want to say
about her eyes, lips, etc., can still be managed. It
turns out she speaks clearly, in German and in
Portuguese. I am now touching her freely. She has
maneuvered so that her forearm is on me.

We are interrupted. It's Carvalho, the Doctor, and
Carvalho's men. They have a tape measure and want
to get the dimensions of Lotte's breasts. I see that the
other girls are already topless. It seems to be a
competition. They ask if I want to do the measuring.
I leave it to the Doctor; he is a scientist. Lotte's
nipples stiffen under his touch. Chairs are pulled up
in a semicircle before us. Some of the girls sit down
also. We are all drinking *pinga* and crushed lime. It's
deadly. I get Lotte to button her sweater and put my
arm around her. How sweet, exclaims the *pipi*-room
matron, little lovebirds—like an engaged couple!

A lapse of time, during which I notice nothing
because Lotte is kissing me. Her breasts burn holes in
my shirt. Then she stops and says it's terrible, she
will never do it, not even with me. I look where she
is pointing. One of the girls, now quite undressed,
has broken out of the other room, followed by
Carvalho, the engineer, and the Doctor. She and

Carvalho are screaming at the *pipi*-room lady. The
engineer is complaining in English, so I begin to
understand. When the Doctor joined him and
Carvalho on the girl, it hurt. She is willing to go back
with two, but not three, and that's what they do.

The pool is lit. Around it, shadows numberless.
Emerald waves when Lotte dives in. She is a good
swimmer. I think I see the triangle of her hair when
she turns. Back and forth, back and forth, there is no
reason why she should ever stop. Carvalho's men are
making too much noise. Drunken giggling. Soon,
some guest will call the reception to complain, but
not yet; no light switch has been turned; the windows
look on blindly. The Doctor tells me he takes care of
these girls' mouths. Doesn't make them pay—
couldn't afford to, anyway. He assures me they are
clean: like young cows. A good mouth means good
digestion.

Lotte is at the metal ladder. I rush to her side with
a tablecloth I have snatched from our table. Don't
want the others staring through verdurous glooms. At
once, she enters my mouth.

The Doctor reproves me for having covered her.
It's foolish, he says, running his hand over her
shoulder. You are treating her like a debutante. She is
here for the guests to share. You leave Rio
tomorrow. She will be coming to many parties.

I know that, but something is tugging wildly at my
heart. An absurdity. Until the thing is consummated,

where is the difference between a virgin and a whore?
I pull Lotte to her feet. While she staggers in her
high heels, looking for her bra, her comb—I see that
her worn-out pocketbook is broken—the laughing
Doctor and I shake hands. Then, cautiously, up the
back stairs, I lead Lotte to my room. Private
policemen with truncheons watch over the dignity
of my part of this hotel. I don't want to tangle
with them.

She likes papaya, and coffee with milk and sweet
rolls. She is very clean. The Doctor is right. Her
mouth is fresh like a mountain source. I am inside it
when the phone rings. A woman's voice, speaking
German too fast for me to understand. I disengage
and hand the receiver to Lotte. Long conversation,
which makes me think of Paul and his sense of
timing. It's my lady of the *pipi* room. Lotte tells me
she is coming up to be paid. She is miffed because
Carvalho left the hotel without paying and she has
had to go looking for her girls' customers from floor
to floor.

I don my bathrobe and meet her in the living
room. She asks for a pittance—hardly worth making
this house call—and I ask that she repeat the figure. I
understood correctly, so I give her vastly more and
say I will be keeping the girl for some days.

My Lotte wants to go to the hairdresser and also
home to get her bikinis and heavens knows what else
before we set out for Angra. I tell her by all means to

have her hair done and to buy the rest at the beach shop downstairs and offer to come with her if necessary. She seems quite pleased by the idea of shopping.

The plane—like a gracious water bug—waited for them at the old airport named for the aviator Santos Dumont just beyond the Praia do Flamengo. The man checking the passports and the pilot, businesslike in a gray suit, gave Lotte curious looks, and Ben half regretted that she had bought anonymous jeans and a shirt to wear on the plane. Contrary to his feeling the evening before, he would have liked to exhibit her such as he knew she was—in her tart's skirt and platform shoes. Dressed in white jeans and a white cotton shirt, carrying the white leather duffel bag into which he told her to put the rest of her belongings, she looked like any girl from Ipanema, unless there were dead giveaway signs that a native's ear or eye would detect independently of dress—her accent? scarlet lipstick and long fingernails to match? And that was not what he wanted. From rooftops, if possible, *urbi et orbi*, he would have liked it proclaimed that he, circumspect and fastidious Ben, was going on holiday with a call girl procured by a Nazi dentist, that he would mount her until they both groaned with exhaustion, and then, lying by her side, he would stroke her fat white rump while she taught him bad little girl's secret German words for each thing they had done or would soon do.

The shoreline passed in review under them. He recognized the end of the beach at São Conrado and soon the plane veered to the right to follow the strange long sandbar of

Marambaia. They had entered the Bay of Sepetiba; their destination was at its western end, across from the Ilha Grande. The plane was flying so low that Ben could see each wrinkle on the water, the smoke rising from occasional chimneys on the tiny green islands that did not appear even as dots on the pilot's map. Lotte squealed—was it fear or excitement?—each time the plane lurched. There was a strong wind, offshore. Then the pilot pointed and Ben saw the landing strip. It was a narrow rectangle of red earth, surrounded by red-earthen walls on three sides, smoothly carved out in the side of the mountain that closed the bay. The plane headed suicidally for the wall at the far end, quickly turned, and came to a trembling halt. Heavy, moist heat enveloped them as they stepped out. A Volkswagen bus was waiting, its windshield covered by red dust.

Their room, itself whitewashed, was at the end of a long white building. Under voluminous mosquito netting stood a narrow bed. A trickle of tepid, brackish water ran from the shower. There was a chest of drawers, a black wooden table, and two black wooden chairs. The driver of the bus, who had taken them to the room, assured Ben that no other rooms, with large beds, were to be had. On the way they had passed through the dining room, with long tables being prepared for dinner. There was but one service, at eight. In the combination bar and salon, dozens of overweight parents and children were gathered before a television set that, although turned to what seemed maximum volume, could be heard only with difficulty in the noise of conversation. When Ben asked for a drink to take to the room, the waiter produced a bottle of beer and a bottle of mineral water. There was wine to be had, but not before dinner. Although Carvalho's description, to which the Hotel do Tio had so far conformed, should have prepared him for this, the feeling of having made a mistake descended upon Ben—in his case usually the precursor of guilt, depression, and anger. He began to wonder whether he could make the plane return for them that very evening. It could take them to Cabo Frio—the same distance from Rio, only in the other direction. There was nothing to stop him, for that matter, from taking Lotte to Uruguay, to Punta del Este, or, since one did not absolutely have to be on the beach, to Buenos Aires. At least he would be offering her something that she might like, that she was not accustomed to. Afterward, she could go back to Rio and he would fly directly to New York. Beginning to plan how to explain these choices to her in German with all the consequential complexities of transportation, and to enlist her in translating into Portuguese the necessary instructions to be given at the hotel and over the telephone, he turned in her direction. She had taken off her shirt and her shoes. The window of the room gave on the sea. She was standing before it, crying very quietly. What is the matter? he asked her. I am so happy, she replied, this room is beautiful. I want to stay here forever.

IN THE MORNING Ben found out that all the motorboats and sailing dinghies belonging to the hotel had been rented or reserved. Only one beach could be reached on foot: it was meager and already covered with the bodies of fellow guests. He sensed that Lotte was not a useful intermediary in dealing with the manager. He sought the man out himself and, in a mixture of Spanish and English, explained how highly recommended the hotel had been by Dr. Alvaro de Carvalho of Rio. The name was the right password—Ben wondered why it had not been noted with his reservation and whether, had he used it the previous day, a room with a large bed might not have suddenly become available. He was reluctant to change now, his room having overnight acquired magic characteristics of its own. When the manager returned, it was with a placid old man with huge hands and calloused bare feet. Wellington was a fisherman and porter. He could not let them have his boat because he needed it for his business. But he would take Ben and the *senhorita* to island beaches each morning and return to fetch them at an agreed hour. This suited Ben. He would let the old man choose the desert rock upon which to abandon them. The manager prepared a basket of bread, white Minas cheese, wine, and water.

Wellington explained in words and gestures that the beach they were heading for was the best in the bay, with large trees to offer shade. The island was uninhabited, except for one small farm on the other side, and it had no name. They would not be disturbed. He pointed to a dense jungle of palm trees and ferns rising up from the shining water less than two kilometers away.

They were slow in arriving. The sun was so intense that the boards of the boat burned their feet. Perhaps twenty meters from shore, in shallow water, Wellington put the engine in reverse and brought the boat to a stop. They took their provisions, climbed out, and, legs in the water, waved good-bye to Wellington.

The silky water was warm and translucent. As they waded to the beach, schools of minnows chased one another, and shadows of slightly larger fish flickered over a bottom that seemed half sand and half sticky clay. Multicolored feathers floated on the surface. The beach belonged to birds, which sat in the branches of the trees or circled overhead, raucous and domineering. With a handful of fern leaves, Lotte swept a space clear of the droppings that covered the sand. They put the food in the shade, took off their clothes, and lay down in the water. Later, they swam. When they returned to the beach, two very domestic-looking hens picking insects from the sand looked up startled, then hurried down a path into the jungle. Ben and Lotte followed them. In the middle of a clearing they saw a hut with more hens and a large rooster. So the single habitation was not on the other side of the island, as Wellington had claimed, but quite near, almost within earshot of the beach. Cautiously they approached and looked in through the window, an unglazed opening in the wall. Inside they could see only an army cot, its canvas stained and torn. But there must have been a presence; someone must have filled the basin from which the hens drank. Although they returned to the island each day during the week that followed, they never saw the hens again and did not solve the mystery.

Notaben 401, dated 16/12/70:

> Lotte dozes in the shade. I read in my battered copy of *Les liaisons dangereuses.*
>
> Her right buttock is my lectern. She is so tame that the rhythm of her breathing doesn't change as I turn the pages. Yesterday, as I was reading in the same

position, her innate trust stirred me; so as not to lose my place, I put the book facedown in the sand and entered very gently, from the rear. She was ready. The light upward pressure of my hand on this same buttock was enough to open her. And she slept on.

No, I am not playing Valmont on Robinson Crusoe's island, if I write a mock love letter to V it will not be in a folio I have balanced on Lotte's posterior. The explanation for *Les liaisons* in this place, with this companion, is chaste. Traveling light, always eager to better myself, I settled on this text to help purge my French of anglicisms and Parisian grime and took no other. If as it happens it has been also of assistance twice today in ways that are more to the point here, that is pure good luck.

In fact, my "mechanism" is quite different from Valmont's. A woman he can have he does not want. I am unable to keep my hands, etc., off Lotte precisely because she is so available. I am tempted to add so *passive*, because what she does, and she does plenty, is done solely in response to my need. How long this harmony could last is a question we need not answer.

Example: The moment when my feeling for the Cockney reached that place, low down in my entrails, which is unfailingly stirred at moments of true complicity with another.

We stop at rue du C-M, quite innocently, so I can drop off my briefcase and wash my face before going on to an opening. She precedes me up the stairs to

my bedroom, and I watch her heavy, English rear
with satisfaction. Once in my room, she pulls open
the drawer where my shirts are stored, opens her
pocketbook, takes from it the round, white plastic
case with her diaphragm inside, and places it under a
stack of striped shirts in which pink predominates.

I want it to be here waiting for us, she says.

Faith, hope, and availability.

Notaben 402:

My German has improved steadily during this
week. It's encouraging how such things return.

It's our last night. They serve a surprisingly good
churrasco with fried manioc flour. We drink very cold
beer. She clings to me at the table, her hand always
at my crotch. Our fellow diners, a branch manager of
Banco do Brasil in Belo Horizonte, his brother-in-law
whose profession I haven't figured out, and their
families have stopped paying attention to us or smile
benevolently. As we occupy the only two places at
the head of the table, I help her discreetly open my
fly. Can pleasure be endless?

Later, under the netting, moonlight on our faces, I
ask her how I will find her when I return to Rio. Will
it be soon? she wants to know. I say next year,
probably before the summer, as early as I can arrange
it. In that case, she tells me, she will perhaps still be
in Rio. The Doctor likes to change the girls, so they
seldom stay long. He likes them to be fresh. There

are so many who want to come! This makes my eyes fill with tears, and I inquire where she will go upon being "changed." She doesn't know, probably a club in São Paulo.

Is it a question of money? Can I buy her back from the Doctor or his partners? She doesn't want that. A part of what she earns is set aside in any case, and in a few years she will be able to retire. Then she will send me postcards from Montenegro, near Novo Hamburgo. That's where she would like to live. Perhaps she will even be able to get married, she adds shyly.

Undated draft of letter from Ben to Véronique (translated from the French by me):

Merry Christmas, my love, I am still in Rio, back from a vacation on a desert island set in the greenest water I have ever seen. I was as helpless there as Robinson before the Lord sent him Friday, totally neglecting suntan oils, etc. Result: Very red and very painful back, yes all the way down, and a marked distaste for sitting down.

Are you skiing well? Is Laurent having fun?

It turns out I will have to be in New York for a while (undetermined in its extent) at the beginning of the new year. Office politics. My faithful troops tell me, Father look to your right, look to your left! I will not bore you with the dreary details or names of homoid sharks you do not know. We will be in touch by telephone. Contact with nature has given me new courage: I will dare to call you in the morning, when I think you have returned from Laurent's school. And you can reach me at home or in the office. Don't forget my New York secretary's name—Carl—or that, all spiteful rumors notwithstanding, he is a man!

You may, with your usual tenderness, wonder where I will spend the holidays. I don't know. Surely away from New York. The bustling cheer of one's friends is too hard to bear. Most probably, I will stay here. There are some people from the rural south of this country who have treated me with unexpected kindness. They have no religion, and, in my case, that's just right for this season.

Your
Ben

VIII

HE INVITED ME to lunch at the Veau d'Or. During visits to New York from college, almost twenty years before, I had gone there with my parents, usually for Saturday lunch, before their afternoon subscription concert. It seemed always filled with people just like them: good-looking and hearty, dressed in bold tweeds, greeting friends, making an agreeably boisterous noise. The owner, Gerard, himself voluble, rubicund, and beautifully turned out in lounge suits of refined grays and blues, reigned over the customers and the harassed, dyspeptic Breton waiters with artful ease; his partner, whom I never heard utter a word, perched behind the cash register at the end of the bar. How one was seated, and the length of the prefatory sojourn in the crowded space between the bar and the coatroom, was determined by criteria that assigned little weight to reservations. My parents would spend less time in that purgatory than my father required to down his first martini; with a mocking flourish, Gerard would take his glass and, carrying it himself, lead them to one of the rare tables where the width of the banquette was sufficient for my father's comfort. Less-favored clients were left to marinate in gin for what seemed the length of a three-course meal, only to be seated ultimately face-to-face on hard wooden chairs at tables one-third the size of those Gerard considered appropriate for my parents. I was sorry he did not appear to know me when I asked for Ben; himself, he had not changed much, and I had hoped that this master physiognomist would see through the film with which years of absence had doubtless covered my face. It seemed awkward to mention my name—clearly he was busy—and also futile: the pleasure I had hoped for was to be recognized spontaneously. Instead, I followed him to Ben's table, the one facing the window, where Gerard himself normally took his meals. So, in this place, too, Ben was now a valued habitué.

You are almost fifteen minutes late, he greeted me. Are you in training for my existential role?

He had lost so completely the sunburned look Prudence and I had admired when he arrived from Brazil and told us about virgin Angra that his face was like the flannel of the gray suit he was wearing, only paler in tone, and untidy, which was never true of his clothes. His eyes were bloodshot. I explained that my editor had kept me longer than I had anticipated going over an article and asked Ben if he had a cold.

No, he replied, I haven't been sleeping well, and it's starting to show. Perhaps I'll go back to Rio and put my body in the sun. A good tan covers everything, wipes away all sins.

The waiter arrived with cold mussels, which the Veau d'Or has always offered as soon as one sits down and I can't eat because I am allergic to the mustard in the sauce. Then, for some minutes, we were busy with Gerard, ordering lunch. When Ben introduced me, Gerard said he was glad to see me again and asked about my parents and why they never came to the restaurant anymore. I told him they rarely were in the city but that, sometime soon, I would bring my own daughters to lunch. The idea that I might resume this family habit suddenly pleased me very much. I thought it would also please my parents; it was the sort of thing around which Prudence might organize one of her letters to my mother.

Actually, repentance and absolution, if you can obtain it, would be more suitable than a suntan, although less chic, I said to Ben. You have wrought havoc in my family. Why aren't you in Paris? You told Véronique you were going. On New Year's Eve, you told Prudence and me the same thing. I have just had a letter from Véronique. She says you haven't even written or telephoned to explain what you mean to do.

I hadn't intended to say any of this. I had thought to speak to Ben about Véronique, but later and more delicately. Now I was accusing him, putting forward a view of his actions—Prudence's, actually, and probably shared by the small number of right-thinking persons to whose attention the affair had come—that I knew did not take into account all the circumstances.

That's not fair, he replied. I didn't telephone while she was in Switzerland because I might have gotten Paul. But the day after the one when she told me she'd be back in Paris I called to ask what she had decided and what she wanted me to do: she said she couldn't speak with me. I called again the next day and she only cried. The same thing happened two or three times more, and the last time she asked me never to call again. I wrote asking for an explanation. The answer I got was one of those letters only your cousin Paul knows how to compose in this decadent era. He told me he was writing on Véronique's behalf as her natural protector and was ordering me to respect his honor, her honor, the honor of Laurent, and the tranquillity of his domicile, and above all to stay out of Paris unless I want my rear end filled with bird shot. Jack, he may have even mentioned your honor! I took this to mean that she had weighed what I told her about myself and the disadvantages of living with someone like me and had decided in favor of Paul.

He emptied his wineglass and continued: Probably, it's a wise choice. I might have advised it myself. One might say I almost did. Of course, I am sorry about the havoc.

By the way, he added after another pause, I have refrained from going to Paris not because I am afraid of Paul and his shotgun. I really haven't wanted to be there; besides, it isn't necessary so far as the office is concerned. We have just made my second-in-command, young van Damm, a partner. You will recall I tried to bring that about. Some people in the bank think it would be just as well in that case if I made my return to New York permanent and official.

Véronique had chosen not to mention in her correspondence either those telephone calls or—assuming that it had not been somehow intercepted by Paul and she had been able to read it—Ben's letter asking for an explanation, though she had copied for me parts of the long letter Ben wrote from Rio de Janeiro. If his declarations of love and readiness to live with her were genuine, she wanted to know, how could he choose to wait quietly in New York for a confirming answer? Hadn't she given him all the answers, all the assurances he needed, during the months they were together, and then, when she compromised herself before Paul's entire family, hadn't she declared her love publicly? His place was at her side.

I realized that Véronique's questions were in large measure rhetorical. I knew her enough to be certain she understood Ben's hesitations and the way he transformed them into scruples. She should have been able to handle these ambiguities. But I could not help believing that Ben had intended her to react just as she did. Unless I was horribly wrong on that score, the selectivity of Véronique's account to me of Ben's actions was unimportant, and her uneven behavior explicable by nervous strain and fatigue. Of the two, she was the more vulnerable. I was suddenly appalled by Ben's lack of imagination and his apathy, which verged on callousness, and I told him so with considerable feeling.

He looked at me queerly and said, I am surprised to hear that from you of all people. Have you forgotten the early Sunday morning fireside conversation in Paris? Do you remember my twins, the not-so-little Sarah and Rebecca? I told you then how hard it was to do what had to be done. I told her the same thing, over and over. It was just as hard, perhaps harder, to let a roll of the dice settle the matter—a huge effort, really; and that's what I did when I wrote to Véronique from Rio and asked her to decide how we were to live. If she wanted to bet on me, why didn't she take me at my word? Of course, I took care to point out the risks, the thorns on the rose; there are so many! But that was nothing new.

Ben, I said, examine your conscience. She thinks that first you led her on (these were words I immediately regretted because I knew they were unjust) and then—instead of jilting her outright—you wrote a careful, mystifying letter. You retired behind a smoke screen. She doesn't know how to act or what to think and she is very unhappy. You don't look happy either. If there is a misunderstanding, don't let it become permanent.

He asked me how much I knew about the letter from Rio I was talking about. I answered that Véronique had quoted long paragraphs from it—I could not know what was missing.

There was a silence during which I ate my food rather unhappily. What right have I to go on badgering him? I thought. Am I giving advice to the lovelorn? What if he takes my advice, undoes the work of the last month, and then their lives and Laurent's turn out badly?

How are Prudence and the children? he asked abruptly.

Fine, I said, fine. I described a plan to send my older daughter the next year to a school in Wales, which was recommended as combining a good academic program with first-rate training in equitation. Jane had become a fine rider during the summer, and Prudence wanted her to be able to reach a higher level in a setting more austere than the usual schools in Virginia and Maryland that stress horsemanship. I was secretly happy of the opportunity to relieve the tension developing between Prudence and Jane, and Jane and her younger sister.

Ben had listened to me with a gloomy face, turning his glass back and forth between his thumb and index finger. He interrupted me: So there has been no family crisis, no tonsils, no wisdom teeth to be removed, no painters in the dining room or the pantry to prevent inviting your lonely and freshly uprooted friend to dinner or a Sunday lunch?

It's a fact that you are not very popular right now with Prudence or my parents, I admitted. Prudence doesn't know what to think. You know you are her pet. She would rather not believe that you have taken advantage of Véronique.

Should Prudence consider the possibility that I am the party of whom some slight advantage has been taken? I have been romantic with the lady, generous with the husband, and discreet as an English butler. I don't know for a fact that English butlers are discreet, but that is their reputation. Naturally, nobody bothers to be discreet about me. Then I fail as a stereotype: I don't explicitly jilt the lady, but it is asserted that the nuptial noises I make are not unambiguous. In retribution, my best friend's wife treats me as though I had stolen the family silver.

What choice had I but to tell him that he was exaggerating the significance of Prue's reaction? I even took it upon myself to invite him to dinner the following Sunday or any other night that week he was free. He shook his head and said he would have to seek absolution from my wife some other time; by Sunday he would be again in Tokyo. He launched into the explanation of the financing of a steel mill and a dispute between some Japanese steel companies and the Belgian consortium he had just advised in Brazil, which had stagnated for a number of years but was now before arbitrators. Huge sums of money were at stake. I was too upset to pay close attention. I suppose he was upset too, and that is why he went on with a deadeningly boring tale, to which I listened just enough to understand that, for reasons unrelated to the origins of the quarrel, Ben's Belgian clients, having taken note of the ease of his dealings with the Japanese in

Brazil, had recently asked him to try to negotiate a settlement with their adversaries in Japan.

I will call you at your magazine when I return, he concluded. Meanwhile, tell Prudence and your parents that I am not all black inside—closer to gray, like my flannels.

As we were getting our coats, I saw that he had in the pocket of his coat a folded copy of the *Daily News* and commented on the new direction his reading had taken. He laughed, patted the paper, and handed it to me.

Take it, he said, the story is told better than in the *Times* and in many ways it's quite relevant.

I read the immense headline. Charles Manson and his two disciples had been found guilty of the Sharon Tate murder.

Undated draft of letter from Ben to Véronique (translated from the French by me):

My adorable Véronique,

I lunched with Jack today. He surprised me by talking about you and me. Being apparently in close contact with you, he was in a position to do so in some detail. I had not realized your cousin was so intimate a friend. Is there anyone in your family whose business we have not become? Would it not be wiser to write to me instead? Yet I have not heard from you once, not once since the day, almost a week after I arrived in New York, when I found your letter waiting at my office. In it, two sentences: You have broken me. Your soul is impure.

Why? Because in the letter I wrote to you from

Rio I urged you to be prudent? Because I repeated one more time—tediously, I am sure—the fears that have tormented me? That must be it, unless my instincts and Jack's meddling have misled me. Yet I had never concealed that those anxieties lodged in my "soul" right alongside my desire for you, alongside my love.

Tomorrow I leave New York for Tokyo. I am not sure of the length of my stay. If you consent to see me, I will return by way of Paris. The shortest of messages—Come!—entrusted to my secretary in Paris or New York will suffice to bring me to you.

Your
Ben

There was no such message. Indeed, I believe that Véronique left Ben's letter—if he sent it—entirely without reply. However, she wrote to me again, several times within about ten days, and it occurred to me that perhaps that was the method she had settled on for remaining in contact with Ben. She said that Paul and she were moving to the rue de Varenne. That was a concession to her taste for the Left Bank and the Faubourg Saint-Germain. But she too was making a concession: the house near Arpajon was on the market. They were looking for a place in the Sologne, as murky and melancholy as they could find, where marsh birds would be plentiful and near enough at hand to satisfy Paul. He had offered her a small-gauge shotgun with a beautiful stock and lessons at the celebrated gunsmith's, Gastine Renette. She had accepted.

As soon as he returned from Tokyo and Brussels, for that is where he had gone next, Ben and I had lunch again. It was only a few weeks after the meal at the Veau d'Or; I had called him, having ascertained from his secretary when he was expected, convinced that he would not make the first move and eager to make up what had almost turned into a quarrel. I also had a practical reason, which was to ask him for names of people I might look up in Brazil. My journalistic assignment there was imminent. Over the telephone, he sounded distracted and impersonal; I could not help remembering that he had told me he often read the newspaper while taking unwanted calls. Although at the end of the conversation he apologized for his tone, saying I had caught him in the midst of preparing for a meeting, I was not without apprehension as I waited in the reading room of my club. He appeared, exactly on time, as always, we proceeded to our table, and I saw that I need not have worried: either Ben had not kept a grudge or he had decided to file it away in a remote drawer of his mind. When I proposed dinner with Prudence at home, he accepted at once and said he had presents for the girls—curious Meiji restoration prints of French young ladies of fashion he had found in Tokyo's biggest department store, of all places—and was glad of an early opportunity to deliver them.

His response about people in Rio seemed unenthusiastic. There was, of course, his economist classmate Plinio, married to a kittenish young woman who might have worn her sexual appetite on her sleeve if all her dresses were not sleeveless. Them I must see if possible, but Plinio traveled a great deal. If I cared for a folkloristic visit to the Yacht Club and the

Jockey Club, a playboy businessman called Carvalho would be happy to arrange it. His secretary would send over the addresses and telephone numbers. There was really no one else he could name. Other Brazilians he knew in Rio either were very dreary, concentrated on salting away hard currency in secret numbered accounts, or had all the Swiss accounts they needed and were too complicated and elusive. One couldn't rely on them.

Elusive in their case, he continued, means being given over to compulsive lying—though not especially about their sentiments. If they show you affection, you need not doubt it. It's more like a system. They lie about practical aspects of existence. For instance: X sends you a telex saying he is coming to Paris to see you next week, in part out of boundless desire to be with you and in part because he needs to get away from the daily routine of work, which is undermining his health. You wait for his arrival—possibly plan a small dinner party in his honor. After a series of telephone calls you learn, if you are lucky enough to reach him, that two days before X's telex reached you, he had in fact returned from a month-long stay in New York and will not be able to leave Brazil during the next six months, the excellent reason being that his business partner has been in an automobile crash and is being reconstituted, bone by bone, in Hamburg—which obliges X to stay close to home and mind the shop. Alternatively, X does come to Paris but earlier than expected and together with two business associates. It turns out that the purpose of the visit, planned weeks in advance, is to bid for a particular object at the Salle Drouot, and X will not have time to see you at all, let alone come to your dinner. Or you might ask X if he will introduce you to Z. Great idea, he says, of course he will be delighted to do it right away, after all Z is married to his first cousin! Only the introduction never happens.

I was laughing, but also wanted to put an end to Ben's tirade. Therefore I asked him whether he had identified the cultural or genetic reasons for this behavior.

A part of it, he replied, can't be specifically Brazilian. Most likely, it's a reflection of the acquired prudence of all very rich people: if one doesn't let on where one is or where one will be at any particular time, one is less likely to be robbed, kidnapped, or importuned, and one begins to apply that precept generally. Also, if one does a single favor for a friend, one may later be asked for an infinite series of smaller and greater favors; one learns to discourage such would-be clients by demonstrating right away one's unreliability. But with elegant Brazilians, these tics seem innate: they sound like birds when they talk, and they wish they could, like birds, flap their wings and fly away if one comes too near. The lies are a form of flight.

A little later, I asked him if he had heard from Véronique.

No, he replied, not a word.

I decided to tell him about their leaving avenue rue de la Pompe and Arpajon; during a moment of stupidity—which now intruded on me like a poltergeist whenever Ben and Véronique were concerned—it occurred to me that he might in the future be writing to a wrong address.

Now I am no longer surprised, said Ben, not about Véronique's silence or the real-estate activities, but about being asked to dinner. Peace has returned to your family, and with it all its joys.

Excerpts from Notabens (all unnumbered and undated):

Banished! Well, not exactly. If I in NY correspond with Gianni about the perfect maintenance and functioning of rue du C-M, so that it will be ready to receive Monsieur as soon as it will please him to return, and then in fact do not go there, that's my decision, or so I can pretend. Reality? *Primo,* I would go mad there. Now that she is in the rue de Varenne, we would meet in the morning: she, newly risen from Paul's couch, her cheeks white and rosy, leading little Laurent by the hand to his *cours* two blocks away, her step bold and energetic, buoyed by the thought of the hundred things she will do later in the day, none of which now concern me; between her long, striding legs the domain I no longer inhabit. And I, what can be said of me? Dragging my carcass to the office. *Secundo,* it may be slightly impolitic to go back to Paris just now. Dear old Dwight keeps asking how I see my future. I do not ask, What future? for fear that I will shock the great leader of my great bank. We must at all personal cost avoid that! Lucky, credulous man, knowing a happy childhood—where was it? in Newport? Mount Desert?—he has had a study of the future of us all commissioned and carried out by some very young consulting persons; therein he reads strange matters. The whole is now greater than the sum of its parts, a proposition I used to think had long ago been disproved; but no, this is the new math of banking and management. Team play, he calls it, but I prefer a musical metaphor: I shall henceforth sound new tunes in our office orchestra. Indeed, I am to take a turn at conducting. Were I to insist, a little chamber group could surely be organized for me just as well in Paris, I could saw away at my violin within it, but what do I care about Paris now that I have lost V?

For the nonce, let's savor from a distance the delights of Gianni's spelling. God bless Olivia for reducing the rent. Comical, though, that she should want to spend the season there, in her own? my own? so well-frequented bed.

And this place? Am I under ban of all good men and women?

Second shameful lunch with Jack. Wanted names in Brazil. If only I had dared to send him to the Dentist! Clearly embarrassed to have called me to moral order. Is it possible he doesn't understand what has happened to me? If so, I can't and won't help him. Hardly understand it myself. My letter was what it was, I humiliated V, but that's not the point, I could have made it all right had I wanted to. *Entre nous*, hasn't she liked to be whipped? Instead, I bugged out. Why?

Poor Jack: the stuff about the twins I served up for

him by the dawn's early light in Paris and then at the Veau d'Or is warmed-over twaddle. They have been terrified to come near me for years. I reek of loneliness and loss. V could have been their friend; they would have seen that I can be loved, that I am not menacing. Jasmine and lilies masking a cloaca, a rat trap baited with cheese.

Why?

The words change with my mood, like clouds pushed by wind, the answer remains the same, as given by another, however hard I try to obscure it: "I myself am hell." Form of punishment in that place? Another has said that too: Living without hope in desire.

In desire of what?

To be like Jack—balls, I wouldn't mind being like Paul! Self-centered, self-assured, occupying a rough, masculine place. Concomitants: Tolerance of imperfection, knowing how to seize happiness when it is there to be had, basking in life, not looking the gift horse in the mouth.

Translation, please!

Véronique foolishly, blindly, miraculously wants me, gives me her body, the balm of her tenderness; proclaims my goodness, begs to heal me. Aha, too late, says incubus Groucho Marx, mustachioed lips grotesquely moving mine, the club that will have Ben as a member he will not join!

And even that is not the whole truth. What if my

heart and limbs melt when I enter her, what if she is teaching me to dwell in light, are there not pools of empty blackness in her "peerless eyes"? Does folly, capricious and devouring, have its temple in this "sovran shrine"?

Like seeks like. Beware of folly, Ben: "emprison" not her soft hand. Hightail it to Angra, copulate in the foam with a nymph; then return alone to the certain devastation you yourself have wrought.

IN THE TWINKLING of an eye, Ben had transformed his West Side apartment. It had struck a mournful, early post-Rachel note, he told me: as long as he was in New York, for the moment not living among Olivia's ghosts, he would try for once to live as he chose, surrounded by white sofas and chairs, treading on polished black boards, enjoying the sun that in spring and summer always pours into that apartment. As we gathered at Ben's in the prolonged dusk, the park was at its early summer peak. Lights were already twinkling in the great buildings on Fifth Avenue; the sky was clear and beguiling. There was a light breeze, and the air smelled fresh, if one disregarded the acrid perfume of pollen, dust, and horse manure. Through the open windows we heard bongo drums. The natives had reclaimed their territory.

Ben was giving this weeknight dinner to try out a new stove, he told us. We had meant to bring our daughters, as he had suggested, but at the last minute we couldn't: they said they had too much homework, so that we were alone with him and a young woman I had seen in his company once before; she seemed French, although she spoke perfect English. The time before, at the opera, she had worn a see-through white blouse and nothing underneath it. She was wearing an equally transparent garment this evening, but less frilly, somewhere between white and yellow, like old lace, with a black skirt, perhaps chosen for contrast with Ben's walls and furniture. I wondered if she put rouge on her nipples, for they too stood out. She had every reason to have anticipated the color scheme: it turned out she was an architect. She had, so Ben informed us, supervised his paint-ers, electricians, and plumbers and placed orders for every-thing he had bought for the present installation. It seemed odd that he took care to delineate her role so ungenerously, as though it mattered that the inspiration for this apartment, which after all was just an expression of what we had liked as students, had been entirely his. We drank martinis. Marie-France's voice was all in her throat. She kept running to the kitchen to bring more olives and little bits of pizza she was heating up. At a certain point, Ben asked her to switch on the lights—the blue-gray shade we sat in was turning sad. She leapt up from the sofa to do it, with something like a little noise of excitement. I saw that Prudence noticed it and that Ben made a face, as though to disavow any inference of familiarity or approval.

The *Times* was publishing huge chunks of the Pentagon Papers. Both Ben and I had known Dan Ellsberg in college; I could claim that for a brief while I had been his friend. His involvement with our war machine, his California marriage, indeed the elegant, elongated silhouette of his wife, whom I had seen here and there in New York before they were married, had been on the periphery of my consciousness. Now I was prepared to defend him; in fact I applauded his courage and, for that matter, the courage and determination of the *Times* to stand fast in the face of the onslaught of Nixon's men. I may have spoken of these things at greater length than I had intended. Prudence, of course, agreed, and smiled to tell me how well I had made my point. I had the feeling that Marie-France was waiting for direction from Ben, and Ben remained silent. Prudence finally said, I can't believe, Ben, that you have switched over to Nixon and those dumb generals.

I haven't, he replied, certainly not to Nixon. Anyway, this stuff has more to do with Johnson's war than with Nixon's. I am depressed, because Dan has made the country look even more foolish than usual, while we are still stuck in the war; I'm not sure that looking foolish will help get us out.

Now Marie-France had her cue. She favored respect and good manners and national unity, and very soon we were discussing with animation the new prevalence of bongo drums and skateboards, the ravages of vandals in the park, and the litter in the streets after the Puerto Rican Day parade. Ben placed us at the dinner table. I saw that it was set with silver and crystal and that the napkins had been folded to stand up in cones like clown hats. Marie-France had been at work; this was not Ben's style. He liked shortcuts in the kitchen and no frills in the service unless he had someone like Gianni at hand. She cleared the first course and brought a roast chicken for Ben to carve while she passed the peas and even filled our glasses. I saw that it was making Ben squirm to have a hostess, and I wished I could have pointed it out to her, because she struck me as a nice, bright girl, not unlike Véronique in her good-natured vivacity, though less beautiful and hardly at Véronique's level of elegance; she was too infatuated to read the danger signals herself.

Prudence had told me she thought we could consider what she called Véronique's fling with Ben a closed chapter, and I had come to believe that she was right. My feelings—never simple—about Ben and Véronique had changed with the passage of time; but I had wished them success and had tried hard to dominate a latent jealousy and curb the indecent excesses of my imagination. It could be claimed, as Prudence did, that I had encouraged them. After all, the Decaze marriage was, like all marriages these days, fair game for enterprising tomcats. My sympathy for Paul was not especially vivid. I did not act on the premise that husbands of beautiful wives must stick together; I was too sure of Prudence for that. I really believed that Ben could give Véronique an incomparably more amusing and fulfilling new life if she loved him and if he loved her. There was simply more to Ben than to Paul Decaze. But now he had failed with Véronique, and she and Paul had managed to bear it out. At least I wanted to hope that given another chance, with a girl who was younger, less complicated, and apparently unencumbered by children, Ben would do a better job. So my heart went out to little Marie-France, and, as we stood at the window of the living room with our brandy, I once again wished Ben luck and hoped that a painful and unresolved chapter in his story was over.

Notaben 556 (undated):

Death is approaching me. The certainty that it is so overcomes me at times of greatest peace; I am tempted to say at times when I am almost lyrically happy. For instance, in the bath: the sky is darkening but I have turned out the light; there is no reason to hurry. My body in the water is small, clearly defined; it resembles my father's in odd details—some liverish spots on my hands and arms, the shape of the big toe. I discover more such details each day. At first the resemblance put me off, like the sudden presence of an intruder, but now my resentment has faded. It's not the old man taking over. It's me growing older. The body is finite in its fragility; the thought that these are signs pointing to a final frontier gives me intense pleasure. Warmth and stillness and, like the insistent buzzing of a giant drone, the excited anticipation that all consciousness may end at any moment—right now—with nothing more than a change of temperature in that body, and I begin a happy, drowsy wait for that ending.

Notaben 560 (undated):

Marie-France asks why I do not take her with me when I have to travel. Your work, I answer, I do not wish to interfere with your work. This does not satisfy her. She can arrange to be replaced, released, Lord knows what. Especially if I go to Paris. She would like me to meet her family and friends there, stay with me in my apartment or at the Ritz, tell everyone about us, be like other people. Never. I have demonstrated I am not like other people.

Disappointed, she reaches for me.

Will I have to hurt her so as to ensure that she will leave what's not quite well enough alone?

In the event, she knows that I must go to Geneva for a while and that I will first spend a day or so in Paris. That time in Paris is now her immediate target, although she knows about Véronique.

I want to, I must see Véronique. Why is she with Paul? It's madness: my madness.

TWO DAYS AFTER Ben's dinner party, I drove Prudence and the girls to Vermont and got them settled for the summer, and the following week, on the eve of Ben's departure for Paris and Geneva, I had dinner with him, at his request. He asked if I minded if it was again at his apartment; we would have something cold with good wine. There were to be many restaurants and hotels in his immediate future; since he had gone to the trouble of redoing his apartment he wanted to use it. This time we were alone. During the meal, we talked about my girls. I said I was beginning to see what they would most probably be like as adults. There was nothing in what I saw that I could reprove, but the disappearance of other possibilities of development was in itself depressing. One knew that neither of them was going to be a Margaret Mead or Martha Graham, with all the good and bad that being out of the ordinary implied. They would just be perfectly good young women, similar to dozens one knew, and the best one could hope for would be that they continued along one of those uneventful trajectories.

Ben listened carefully, mostly in silence. We finished the first bottle of his Margaux and started on another over my protests.

Don't worry, he said, either we will drink it all or you will take home what's left. We won't let it go bad.

That made me remember that he was leaving the next day. As he had seemed tense all evening, I asked whether someone who traveled as much as he still felt an undefined anxiety before leaving on a voyage.

I don't know, he said. In my case, it's not anxiety, at least not this time. More like excitement on the eve of battle. There are some difficult things I will have to get done.

Then he told me he had a favor to ask. He had just made a new will and named me his executor; he had been in a hurry and hoped I did not mind that he had not consulted me in advance. His old will was the one he had made while he was still married to Rachel. He had not bothered to change it, because it left essentially everything to the twins, which was pretty much what he still wanted, but the executor was Rachel's lawyer, and he saw no point in continuing that arrangement. I told him that of course I was flattered by his choice, but that I doubted I had the necessary business and legal skills.

Don't worry, Ben said. If I have any money left when I die, you will hire the law firm of one of your classmates to do the work, and the estate will pay both him and you. I want you to have the executor's commission; it's pretax dollars. The only thing you will get under the will is a rather

whimsical bequest. I can't tell how useful it will be to you
by the time you receive it.

Notaben V12 (undated):

Dinner with Jack. He shouldn't drink very great
wine so fast. No point; can't taste it. Tomorrow,
plane for Paris. Should I wait a day before I call V?
Get rid of the headache & tremor of fatigue, go to
her anointed like a bridegroom?

Paid another visit (wonderfully appropriate
expression in this case) to Dr. Durer this morning, he
of the missing umlaut. Six times in the last three
weeks. No change in him since our encounters at the
end of Rachel's Era. Change is for patients; he has
attained nirvana. Same little brown-haired man in a
little brown jacket and black shoes that have never
touched a sidewalk. Not a grain of dust. Puts them on
when he gets to the office; real shoes must be in the
closet. Why not do as the Japanese do? Leave shoes
at door; shuffle off to pee in caramel-colored plastic
slippers. Would make it possible to remove the
transparent plastic from his awful couch, where my
street-soiled footgear comes to rest.

I know nothing about him, not even in which part
of Mitteleuropa he acquired that accent, manly/tender,
like my father's. There must be a Frau Dr. D; surely
she likes crystal boxes and Rosenthal figurines. On
Saturday she takes him shopping for a new fur coat,
keeps him in this impeccable condition. Lucky man.

Had I only stuck to my own kind, might have been like that myself. Don't like my own kind, that's one problem; don't know what my kind is, that's another.

Dr. D listens to my new predicament. Such states of feeling can be treated over a sufficient period of time, he opines gently. You have not taken time to be treated. It may be that you feel safer remaining as you are.

No tone of reproach there. If he were not out of my field of vision in his bentwood rocker, making it go creak-creak, I would probably see a kindly little smile float around the corners of his mouth. So equable; so sure of himself. Like one of those great golfers hitting the ball very far, shown in slow motion.

He continues: I can't advise you how to respond to the French lady. You know that. (Or words to similar effect.) In any case, the outcome is unlikely to be what you anticipate.

He offers Miltown. I accept the prescription and have it filled. Joseph's race: be ready for the lean years.

So much for prophylaxis. Once more, Dr. D and I are in substantial agreement.

IX

Il n'aurait fallu
Qu'un moment de plus
Pour que la mort vienne
Mais une main nue
Alors est venue
Qui a pris la mienne.

The singer crooned, reaching the intractable mass of Ben's
resentments and longings in their sullen hiding place; his
voice—old-fashioned, bewitching—gave them attractive expression, one that Ben thought was, by the sleight of metaphor, weirdly accurate. Alas, he had never managed to do so
well himself during those exhausting moments of sincerity
when he strove to explain to Rachel, in the old days, and
then to me or Dr. Durer his sense of loss and dislocation.
Implacably intrusive, the voice continued:

Moi qui frémissais toujours
De je ne sais quelle colère
Deux bras ont suffit
Pour faire à ma vie
Un grand collier d'air . . .

Yes, that was the desperate and, in his own case, apparently vain longing for the other, into whom one could melt, the other who was the healer.

The scratchy portable "pickup" in Guy Renard's living room was working its way through a record of Léo Ferré singing poems by Aragon. Ben had asked Guy to play it, perhaps because of that song. They were drinking too much scotch. The day had seemed endlessly bright; if the sun ever set, if dusk came, they would go to the Bois for dinner. Navy-blue shade of the huge trees, lamps like fireflies on the gleaming white of round tables, a pink sky smudged with smoke: it was worth waiting for. The record had been a favorite of Guy's and of his band of friends' the summer that Ben first met them in Porquerolles. The funny record player, really like a red, imitation-leather valise, was their inseparable companion. Shocking Ben by their indifference to silence, they took it to coves that could not be reached by land, where one swam off the anchored *pointu*; at his house, when they came in the evening, they would set it on the balustrade that separated the terrace from the rocks and the sea. They sang along with the record—such strong, melodious voices they had, and perfect memory for the words. Slowly, two of the girls would dance together. No light was allowed in the windows of the pink villa—they were serious about stargazing. In a circle around the table cigarettes burned like eyes of cats.

Ben had arrived in Paris that very morning. Right away, he called Véronique. She was in Paris; she had not left for the country; the maid, whose voice he did not recognize, was willing to find out whether she was at home. A long wait, then Véronique came to the telephone. They spoke quickly, out of breath. No, she could not see him today, not at any time. And tomorrow? Yes, tomorrow, she would have lunch with him; yes, at his hotel if he wished it.

Against all probability then, he was to see her, and it was to be on his terms! There had been no recriminations; he had not had to plead his case. His heart beat very hard, and he sat for a while on the bed, near the night table where he had hung up the receiver, with his eyes closed, pressing his hand to his chest as though to calm the organ within it. Afterward, having changed rooms and unpacked—he now dared to acknowledge to himself that this suite with a pretty but totally unostentatious living room, on the courtyard side, away from street noise, would serve him better than the standard room, filled by its twin beds, into which one entered directly from the corridor the hotel had first offered—he got hold of Guy. Another miracle, albeit minor: Guy was free that evening and did not object when Ben declined his offer to find a girl who might join them at dinner to make the table more festive.

So, exalted, just a tiny bit light-headed from whiskey and fatigue, Ben waited for the sky to change to the appropriate color and for the question that would eventually be put, while Guy discoursed, in beautifully orotund sentences, on the patterns into which relationships among their mutual friends (and indeed friends of Guy's whom Ben knew only by name) were currently organized, and thought how much like the Hayden Planetarium this was—a well-trained voice, a velvet sky, the Constellation of the Fox displayed upon it.

And how go the affairs of our little Madame Decaze? Guy asked. Odile tells me you have returned her to the owner.

An unkind interpretation, Ben replied. Her affairs, so far as I am concerned, are in suspense, by her own design.

It would have been better for her if she herself had managed to convey that impression. For reasons one cannot understand, she has chosen the role of the victim. Is it a specially refined taste for public humiliation or natural naïveté? Impossible to say—perhaps it's her American education. On the other hand, most members of the Decaze family are naturally malevolent. They must like having her in the role of the mistress you rejected; it puts her under their thumb.

I am seeing her tomorrow, said Ben. Tomorrow, we may change roles.

Notes on the back of the menu for lunch on July 7, 1971, from the grill of the Crillon in Paris:

> Waiting for Véronique. Came down here early on purpose; make sure of decent corner table. By my count only four of these deserve the name. Better to look at her from the side, especially her ears. Then take her hand; knees might touch, tentatively.
>
> Portrayed on these avocado walls by some Hungarian's hand are horses and jockeys at Longchamp. The race is about to start. What will be the purse for the winner at my table? Her heart? My life?
>
> Guy was tactless by design. He cares for me and so

does Jack, only Guy understands better the necessary rules of mating. I knew what he would say, could have given the easy advice myself: stay away from trouble, never try to fix a botched suit (pax, Monsieur Jeanne), misery loves company and it's company you do not need. But what if he and I—and Dr. D—are wrong, and V and I miss the one and only wave that can carry us to shore? Will I say then: *Par prudence* (by Jove, no pun intended) *j'ai perdu ma vie?*

Hush, Ben. Here she comes.

She wore a summer dress that was new to him: a stiff, navy-blue cotton affair, with a white pinstripe and a shirt collar. Like a shirt, unbelted, it buttoned down the middle. Instinctively, he disliked it: it was not the sort of thing one would have expected a woman like Véronique to choose for a lunch such as this. Did she think she was stopping at the Crillon for a quick bite with him between a morning of shopping and an afternoon appointment at the dentist? It had to be the dentist, not the hairdresser, her hair was cut very short—freshly mowed, he would have been tempted to blurt out—and clung to the skull like a gold-and-silver casque. This too irritated him, as though he should have been consulted before this step had been taken, or at least given warning of its consequences. And she carried some sort of awkward parcel, from Aux Trois Quartiers, and now was resolutely resisting the headwaiter's efforts to remove it from her grasp. There was no need for more proof! Since she was to be in the place de la Concorde at one, she had decided to run a convenient errand beforehand. Monstrously, slowly, the thought began to form in his head that he might have misread the script from the start—it could be that this had always been a one-man passion play, with no female lead role in it at all—or more likely, that feelings and events having organized themselves for Véronique on an accelerated schedule far in advance of his own, the script he thought he knew had been definitively discarded and replaced.

Ben, what are you doing in this hotel? Has Olivia thrown you out? Has the Ritz closed its doors? She held out her hand.

Olivia continues to think I am a perfect tenant, and to reinforce that opinion I have given her back her house until the end of the month. She wants to enjoy the Paris season. The reason I am in this place is that my senior partner, his wife, and countless children and cousins are at the Ritz to cleanse their shirts and bodies after pony trekking in Iceland. Dwight told me that if I happened to be in town at the same time as they, he would like us to have a meal or two together. I decided I would stay out of sight. So here I am, with half of the American press and all the State Department types for whom there was no room at the embassy. The peace talks must be at a delicate point or else, like Olivia, they all wanted to enjoy the Paris season.

She said, Ben you are unchanged. You talk to prevent silence and you listen to yourself. What happened to us hasn't marked you.

Just what has happened, he asked, will you please explain it to me? If you liked me as I was, why aren't you glad I am still the same? That's what I came to Paris to find out. Of

course, I've noticed changes in you: you don't answer my
letters and you have cut your hair like a boy's. Are the two
related?

Ben, stop playing with words. It's childish and unfair and
I am famished. Please order lunch.

He consulted the menu and the waiter. She did not speak
except to tell him she did not want wine. That's another
change and also a bad sign, he observed. Are there many
more I should expect?

She said, When you were in Brazil, you abandoned me. I
had written to tell you what I had done. You knew I had
done it so there would be no way out: we would have to be
together. And still you turned me down.

A tear began a long descent down the side of her nose,
followed by another. Then she was crying very hard. Ben
disliked public display of emotion. He watched in silence.
She stopped eating, sniffed into a handkerchief, dried her
eyes and cheeks, and said, I am not sure what difference it
can make, but I have come to receive your explanation.

He undertook to give it. His mouth was dry, although he
drank glass after glass of water and then of wine. Against the
pleasant obligato of the busy dining room, he heard his own
voice rise and fall interminably—mechanical, off-key, absurdly distinct, and unlistened to—as though he had been
moved mistakenly to make an unwelcome, ambiguous, and
overly long toast at a banquet where his presence was in
itself a mistake. His French was out of control; for the first
time since they met, he began to address her in English, to
exclude any error in nuance or connotation.

He knew he was telling her things she had listened to

many times before, he said: his failure with Rachel and the twins; how the loneliness that always dogged him turned into shame in the sexual act, because sterility rendered the act futile and as sinful as Onan's; that she had brought to him a vision of such new possibilities of sunny happiness that he felt he must hold his breath and remain very still lest the vision fade. These were the reasons, he told her, for the vacillation, the constant hanging back—mistrust, sometimes loathing of himself, never lack of love.

Poor Ben, she said and put her hand over his. Now you have explained the first letter. But what about the second? How could you have written that one—so callous, so wounding? Why did you not come back to Paris? Tell me what happened between the two letters.

The waiter brought his grilled sole. He watched him bone and reconstitute it with quick movements, arrange it on the plate together with the perfectly formed steamed potatoes, before the fish could cool. No, he didn't want the beurre blanc, not even on the side. He tried a small piece of the fish; it was perfect, it had always been perfect, one could suppose it would be perfect each time in the future. The conjugation was endless. Véronique was eating steadily, her eyes fixed on her plate. She must have told the truth when she said she was starved.

First I went, quite unintentionally, to a sort of orgy, he said, and then, quite intentionally, I took a short, idyllic vacation with the nicest of the girls I met at the orgy. When I returned to Rio de Janeiro, I wrote that second letter. I did not think I could return to you straightaway.

I want a description.

As he complied, he noticed that his voice had returned to normal and that he was telling the story well, as he might have told it to me. A large erection was tugging at his trousers. Véronique had stopped eating. She did not resist when he took her hand.

You enjoyed being with a whore, she said. That is what you really wanted. You should have come to me immediately. I am better than your Lotte. I do everything. I have always wondered about the things you did not ask me to do, why you never beat me. You know one can. Can we go to your room now? Isn't that why you had me come here?

When she took off that offending dress—unbuttoning it, her fingers were ahead of his—he saw that she had nothing underneath, not even stockings. She stood before him waiting, eyes downcast, her feet red instead of pink where her shoes had pressed against them, stomach delicately veined and oddly round, like Dürer's Eve. He put his hand on her belly button and caressed it.

You can feel its head, she said, guiding him. It has even begun to kick. And then, pushing his hand away, do it to me hard, as hard as you can, from the back, right here, in your clothes. I am all hot. You have kept me waiting.

Except for the hoarse cooing of the pigeons on the wire mesh that was stretched over the courtyard to keep them off windowsills, no sound reached the bedroom. She had torn the stately covers from the bed. They were on the floor now, a wrinkled, ancient mountain. The wall on the other side of the courtyard glowed yellow in the late afternoon sunlight. Where they were, in the shade, the light was still very bright

but cold. Véronique had pulled up the blanket over them.
Head in the hollow of Ben's shoulder, she was asleep. She,
too, had told her story.

By some quirk both of Ben's letters had reached her in
Verbier on the same day, and after she had read them she
decided to return at once to Paris, alone. She had no clear
idea of what she would accomplish in Paris. Try to reach Ben
through his secretary? Take a plane to Brazil in the hope of
finding him? Wait for a telephone call or the next letter,
telling her that he had been drunk, that she was not to worry?
Perhaps there was nothing to be done at all, but she thought
she could not continue to tremble so and stay in Laurent's
and Paul's presence and be on show in the chalet at evening
meals. She told Paul she was bleeding at the wrong time and
was scared. Fear of unknown gynecologists was something
even he could sympathize with, and the panic she felt about
Ben made it easier to convince him of her distress. The snow
was excellent. He agreed to stay with Laurent and the baby-
sitter until the Monday after New Year's Day, just as had
been planned.

The planes from Geneva were full; she waited in the airport
for a cancellation and finally got a seat on the last evening
plane, in the last row of the tourist cabin. She was exhausted
and fell asleep immediately at takeoff, only to be wakened a
few minutes later when dinner service began. Next to her, on
the aisle side, sat a man not fat but of enormous size: his
arms, his thighs, overflowed in her direction. She refused the
meal and asked instead for a blanket and began to doze again.
When slowly and reluctantly she awakened she felt a warm

thing, huge and insistent prying her legs open, stroking her, making her horribly wet, then going inside, exploring, withdrawing, returning, pinning her down with irresistible weight. She opened her eyes, the man winked and then smiled pleasantly, and with his left hand lifted his glass to her. His right arm, she saw it, in shirtsleeve, was buried up to the elbow under her blanket, moving slightly, while what she understood were his fingers had enlarged their activity, another one now penetrating her at a lower place with slow pressure until the wall between these intruders seemed to have been grasped by a cautious, relentless clothespin. His elbow pressed against her belly, below her ribs, knocking out her wind. There was no resisting it. She came in bursts so violent she bit her arm not to cry out. At once, the hand responded. Quiet now and fraternal, it retreated gently to her furry part, which it scratched, patted, and comforted, like the head of a cat.

For the first time, he spoke. It was to say he had only begun. He called her *ma cocotte*. While his tray table was cleared and folded, the attendant bending over him, the fingers descended again imperturbably, as though familiar with the terrain, more rapid, their demands capricious and larger, growing, she thought, as he drank his brandy and she writhed.

They spent the night in the hotel at Orly. He was Swiss, traveling to Stockholm; the connection was early; he had no need for sleep. From his suitcase, an aluminum box really, he took a camera and a folded tripod. There was an envelope of color photographs. He showed them to her, one by one.

On certain of them, he identified the woman. A large number were of his wife. When he paused, it was to enter her and ejaculate almost immediately. Toward dawn, when she was so sore her juices ran pink, he took pictures of her alone and also with him, before the tripod. Later he showed her how to work the camera and shoot him with the focus on his face. It grinned above the member he held in two fists, like an eyeless trout.

It's your fault, you bastard, she hissed at Ben, you broke me, you made me do it. He was nothing, just a monstrous machine you sent. He smeared and mashed me and now it's your turn and you are so small you don't even fill me.

She left the bed and rushed from one end of the room to the other, with her hands twisting the ends of her breasts or pounding her stomach.

Abruptly, she became completely calm, sat down beside Ben, and stroked his face. The child is that man's, she said. I hadn't been sleeping with Paul. As soon as I realized I was pregnant, though, I got him to do it. I said I wanted it so badly I couldn't sleep; he could pretend I was someone else if he was still angry at me. It takes time with him, but I can always make him do it when I want to. Now I will make you do it and when you go soft I will make you do it some more. I want to be pink again, like underdone veal.

Note on Crillon stationery (undated):

Ravaged bed, inexcusable stains on the blanket. Called the housekeeper, had it all changed. Flowers too. In the mirror, weary face, leech marks on sides of neck and arms. Quite unpresentable, but am I going anywhere?

Awake at last she says, as though a sponge had passed over the blackboard: Was it all right?

Later, What now, Ben? Will you take me, with the baby? Don't forget: you made this child, that man only laid me.

Once more calls me a bastard and latches on—hard.

Still later, sky turning white, she asks me to order tea. What about my question, Ben?

She is wearing my suit trousers and pajama top; unbuttons the top; says soon she will have milk; will I want her to squeeze it in my tea?

Her question. It occurs to me that the answer will make no difference. It might as well be yes so that is what I say.

Howls of laughter—wish it had been demonic, but no, just laughing her head off. Just barely manages to get the words out, she is shaking so hard all over: You are late, Ben, seven months late!

She took the night train to Biarritz.

X

AND AFTERWARD?
It would be pleasant to report that Ben traveled widely, visited countries difficult and perilous of access, paused before exotic landscapes and celebrated ruins, knew other loves and other disappointments, until at last, weary and yet, in his growing indifference, more tolerant, he learned to accept from a companion the viaticum of serenity—perhaps even happiness. That is not how it turned out.

He left Paris for Geneva the next day, took care of his business there, and returned briefly to New York. I was still in the city, alone. It may be that he tried to reach me at home while I was out; certainly he left no message at the magazine. One more trip to Geneva took place in July. He passed through Brussels, for meetings in his clients' ornate, almost deserted headquarters building. All he had done on their behalf in the previous meetings with the Japanese parties— the concessions he had proposed and the ones he had obtained—gained approval. The talk was slow, with endless summaries of what had already been exposed, as specialists were called in successively to state their opinions; out of ingrained habit, and to prevent his eyelids from closing, Ben scribbled in his notebook. During pauses in the deliberations, he stood before the huge windows of the boardroom and stared at the royal palace on the other side of the avenue. The Belgian flag was high on the mast. Somewhere inside that building, therefore, were the childless king and queen and their courtiers with complicated, harsh-sounding names, just like the names of these cordial bankers, reminders of lost provinces and tales of chivalry.

In Geneva, he found the Japanese group less certain of its positions than before—evasive, seemingly ready to put all previous informal agreements in question; a New York lawyer, unknown to Ben, had been added to the Japanese team. During an acrimonious negotiating session, while his employers chattered among themselves in Japanese, he challenged Ben's tax assumptions, and, what seemed more grave, the relationships to be created after the settlement took hold, all of which Ben had considered adopted, at least in principle. These were the essential elements of the settlement. But Ben had had his bank's law firm study the tax issues the New York lawyer seized upon, and his understanding of them had been confirmed; he thanked his stars and his solid early training for having taken that precaution. Telephone conversations ensued with New York and then among teams of lawyers assembled in New York; the work in Geneva was suspended, yet no one dared leave lest departure be taken to signal the collapse of the negotiations. Ben watched over his clients and their morale, determined to prevent premature compromises.

Several days passed in this manner. It was very warm. Toward the evening, Ben visited antique shops in the Grand'Rue and along the streets adjacent to the cathedral, knowing there was nothing he wished to see or buy. He kept thoughts of Véronique at bay, until her image appeared only at an impossibly vast distance, as though of a dancer trembling, on pointed toes, at the center of a brilliant and icy stage, perceived through the converging lens of opera glasses. Finally, the New York lawyer declared himself satisfied with Ben's initial construct; the feeling of relief was general, and plans were made for meetings at which all remaining outstanding items would be resolved and the final documents signed. The meetings would begin on August 3. That left enough time for Ben to spend a few days in New York. The bank's lawyers would come to Geneva to work on the documents; he needed to see them beforehand to go over various problems. In addition, he wanted van Damm, from his Paris office, to be present, as well as a financial specialist to verify projections both parties had been making. In van Damm's case, this implied finding a New York partner to replace him in Paris while he helped Ben. Europe was changing. One could no longer confidently leave an office unattended in August, counting on the month-long sleep of finance and industry.

This time, I was at home when Ben telephoned. I suggested that we meet for dinner, but he said that was impossible. It occurred to me that he was with Marie-France in the evenings and preferred not to have me tag along. Surely that was what I hoped. We settled on lunch at the Veau d'Or. The place was uncharacteristically empty. It would be closing for the summer vacation in a few days; Gerard, in fact, had already left for France. We were greeted by a nod and some inaudible phrase of welcome from Gerard's mute partner. A harassed and badly shaved waiter showed us to the same table as on the previous occasion. I asked Ben whether he had seen Véronique in Paris. He replied, Yes, but that was weeks ago, and offered no comment. As I had not heard from her at all, I might have pressed for some hint of what had taken place, but Ben abruptly changed the subject.

Have you by chance read any Jouve? he asked. I don't know if he has been translated. The novels are beautiful and transparent. You won't have any difficulty. Read *Le monde désert*: it's the last word on what may happen when one has been soiled.

I told him I had not even heard of Jouve and wondered what he meant by this subject at which this author excelled.

A condition worse than dishonor or disgrace, Ben replied. You always make me correct my English, and quite rightly so. In English, "soiled" is probably the wrong word, because it suggests dirt at the surface. I should have said "defiled."

There was a silence. A feeling of shapeless worry—but it may have been only curiosity and the pleasure I had always taken in talking with him about books—impelled me to return to Jouve. Why should you and I be particularly interested in defilement and works on this subject? I asked.

I am not ready to tell you that, Ben replied, but I will tell you something about this novel.

Imagine a writer with a head like a large egg, just a bit darker than the usual sort of supermarket white, on which a clever hand has drawn eyes, wire-rimmed glasses, and a long nose—really a Jouve look-alike, called Pascal. Luc Pascal, not Blaise. Enviously, secretly, Jouve lurks also in the protagonist, Jacques, the son of a great Geneva divine. Jacques is gorgeous, a Nordic Narcissus who can't keep his hands off little boys. The feeling between Luc and Jacques is very strong—the sort of exaggerated pre–World War I friendship that leads two men to spend long summer holidays in Alpine chalets or cottages on the seashore, with room enough for one to write and the other to paint or compose music. Although it might have fitted the story, there is no sexual attraction between them; none anyway we are authorized to infer. Ostensibly, it's because Luc loves only women; I think the better reason is that Jouve will not allow himself to be on view.

As the genre requires, between the two friends stands a woman, Baladine, Russian of course, beautiful and large breasted. To Jacques she is mother, sister, and wife. Luc desires and then loves her. She will yield to his desire, but he does not possess her until it is no longer a seduction; he waits for her to accept the act entirely. Jacques has a presentiment that the irreparable is about to happen: treason, the gravest sin God is called upon to punish.

So Luc and Jacques are defiled by Luc's treason and his jubilation in it. Now comes Jacques's turn to defile Baladine. Although for him women are nothing but a repugnant sack, he takes her. He uses her money; he buys refined, provocative clothes—to attract boys—and after the boys he returns to her.

You do know Geneva? he asked me. I had been listening in silence and replied that I did.

Then you will remember the cliffs between the place where the Rhône pours itself into the lake and the junction with the Arve. Imagine a night in November. Turbulent, black water, the bise blowing very hard. Jacques is running toward the great bridge. Jouve has him make a funny noise: Tsic-Tsic.

Djag-Rag. Perhaps Jacques only hears it. He halts just beyond the bridge; measures the height of the parapet. It's a
good place. He will attain Unity with God. A few days later,
his bloated body is found on the herse that guards the river
turbines.

Although the book is a small masterpiece, I find what
comes after the death mannered and not very interesting. No
wonder; what was there left to say? Even Tolstoy doesn't
have an easy time sustaining the story after Anna has jumped
under the train.

I will read Jouve's book, perhaps this summer, I told him.

Do, he said, if I have time I will send it to you so that you
will have it in Vermont.

The rest of the conversation was about my wife and daughters and the small incidents of their summer in the country.
That was the last time I saw Ben. A few days later, he left
for Geneva.

Note on Swissair stationery, dated August 1, 1971:

> Véronique thinks she has been defiled by her
> neighbor on the airplane; she takes me for the
> effective agent of that event. That's perfect nonsense.
> Distress over my letters, confusion about the future,
> even my behaving like a cad (if in fact I did)—none
> of that should have caused her to submit to that
> man's caresses (all she had to do was slap his face
> and call the stewardess), or to follow him to the
> Hilton, or, strangest of all, to bear his child in order
> to bring him up as Paul's. She told me that once—

before Paul—she had had an abortion. To be sure, she spoke of it with resentment—at the French legal system that denies women contraceptives—but not as if the event had a tragic quality.

In fairness, it is I who have reason to feel defiled: by the role she has cast me in, and by the way she used me during that afternoon at the Crillon.

There is no consolation to be gotten from logic or rules of fair play. The point is, I have thrown away my chance with her. It's beyond repair. Suppose she changes her mind: Would I, who had not begged her on my knees to come to me with Laurent (never mind whether my tergiversations were really about him), take her with the little Hilton she is carrying now? Never. Would she want any such thing? No. That child's destiny has been traced: to be her secret ally in unending revenge she will take on Paul and on me.

It need not have happened. While she lost her head, I kept mine. What was the use of being so cautious about what I might think of her and she of me in the future? As it is, I have thrown away a pearl richer than all my tribe. Ever mocked by metaphors. Othello had no tribe, just a goddamn handkerchief; I have nothing and nobody. Such as Véronique was, she made me happy as no one has except Rachel. Before she began to press me to act like a normal man, she made me a good deal happier. The poor dummy actually loved me. Rachel knew better: her idea was that, for a time, I could love her on a live-in basis. Probably that is all I am good for, although for a while, with Véronique, I made progress—I was beginning to be able to bear it, without wincing, when she was nice to me. No mean trick, as Marie-France and her many colleagues would attest.

What does Jouve have Jacques say? *Je suis dans le désert. Le monde se sépare de moi. À cause de mon péché.*

Phil Norris's law firm had always served Ben's bank. He was the partner who joined Ben in Geneva; they had often worked together in the past. I have known Phil since Exeter; during my last year in school he used to come up from Cambridge together with other alumni who had gone into the war directly after graduation and then in '45 or '46 were freshmen in college. Within limits imposed by his professional discretion, it was easy for me to ask what he remembered about Ben in Geneva. I have also had long talks with Scott van Damm about those meetings and related subjects. They agreed that Ben's was a virtuoso performance.

That he should have a complete grasp of the structure of the settlement and the new undertakings the parties were embarking upon was not surprising; he was their principal architect. They were both struck, however, by his mastery of technical details buried in the hundreds of pages of legal writing that gave effect to the agreements and by the penetration with which he assessed the consequences of changes developed in the course of laborious drafting sessions. The work went on late into the night, each day, without stop, including the weekend. It was normal—indeed necessary, given his high personal standing and role as the originator of the settlement—for Ben to break off for some hours in the evening. Depending on where he was needed more, he would either dine alone with his Belgian clients to review the day's progress and prepare the positions to be taken on open issues, or bring the leaders of the two groups together over a meal in an effort to find solutions, in relative privacy, for problems too delicate for discussion in general meetings. There translation into Japanese interrupted the flow of ideas and the presence of a larger audience incited negotiators on both sides to advance rigid and unrealistic proposals. After dinner, however, he invariably returned to join the working group and did not leave until he was satisfied that the day's decisions had been accurately reflected in the papers and that all difficulties and inconsistencies encountered during the process of drafting, which did not require additional substantive negotiation, had been resolved. Ben had a reputation—on the whole deserved, according to both Phil and van Damm—for a sort of fastidious remoteness and impatience, which, again according to them, did not endear him to younger colleagues and lawyers obliged to work on his transactions, however much they might respect his talent. During this period he showed the other side of his nature, so well known to me: he was, as Phil put it, gentle and affectionate with the working group, quick with praise, tolerant even when, with an uncanny instinct, he went straight to errors in drafting or calculations, displaying a hitherto unknown irreverent gaiety that lifted their spirits. Upon the closing of the settlement, the sense of relief, mixed with wonder at what had been accomplished, was general. After congratulatory speeches, as champagne corks were beginning to pop, a long round of applause for Ben came spontaneously. He had become every-one's hero.

This was on the morning of August 11. It was therefore possible for the Belgians, for van Damm, and for his assistant, to get away to join their families for the crowning weekend of the summer. The Japanese group was bound for Tokyo, Phil for Wyoming, to resume an interrupted vacation. By lunchtime, like guests at a party that had gone on too long past midnight, seeing the waiters finally move bottles and glasses off the bar, they scattered.

Ben lingered in the hall of the Hôtel des Bergues. After the last handshake, when he had seen all of them off, it occurred to him that willy-nilly he would have lunch alone. As there was no hurry, he went upstairs first, to his room in the corner of the second floor, and looked out at the trees and the river glistening blue and white in the sun. Even his room was warm; he supposed that outside, in the city, the heat was intense. On the table and on the chest of drawers lay drafts he had worked on the night before and first thing that morning. They were no longer needed; their arid pres-ence in the room suddenly irritated Ben. He rang for the chambermaid and asked her to take the documents away and to see to it that they were thrown into the trash at once—he remembered that they were confidential and that, in theory, he should have given them to one of the young lawyers charged with retrieving every scrap of paper. Faced by the newly unencumbered surfaces, the woman began to arrange on them the customary publicity display: visitor's guides to Geneva, advice about the opening hours of the two hotel restaurants, and an invitation to deposit valuables in the safe.

He stopped her brusquely with a reminder that it was his habit to throw such things daily into the wastebasket. The room was becoming intolerable. The chairs and side tables crouched on the pale pink rug in a circle—beasts ready to leap as soon as he turned his back, the odiously small colored engravings of the Alps hung too high and crooked. He felt his skin tingle with nervousness, tension, and fatigue. It was like the torment of long insomnia. He called the chambermaid again, gave her a tip, and told her to put flowers in place of the papers she had removed.

A German couple was seated at one of the tables in the windowless bar, where he stopped on his way to lunch; he chose a bar stool from which he could watch them. They were married. Both had new, expensive clothes and leather accessories that were somehow similar; had they been bought at the same store? He studied the woman's maroon pocketbook, odd for August, and matching pumps, never walked in, like Dr. Durer's. The man smoked. His cigarette holder, case, and lighter were gold; he wore a suit of pistachio gabardine. From time to time, he stroked the woman's calf. They were drinking brandy. Obviously, they had eaten an early lunch. Ben supposed this was the prelude to a siesta. The way they spoke about Geneva, they could not have known each other very long. Most probably a second marriage: comfortable people, with money in their pockets, glad to be in this very comfortable hotel. There was no use drinking a second martini in order to outwait them. What would he find out? Follow them upstairs, discover which room they were in? Childish games for lonely travelers, he thought, played too many times. Having lunch in the more formal of the two restaurants, which adjoined the bar, similarly windowless and serving resolutely French food, repelled him. He decided to eat in the hotel café, which opens on the quai des Bergues, and to drink a bottle of Valais red with the meal. Later, although alone, perhaps he too could sleep.

Europe's canicular August 15 weekend, which empties cities, sending to the mountains and beaches all but the bed-ridden, cantankerous doctors, and pharmacists sufficiently unlucky or unimportant to be designated for emergency duty, was upon him. He had made no plans to leave Geneva, any more than to stay for a particular length of time. As he had explained to his clients, this was a part of his usual tactics in a negotiation: instead of presenting the adversary with a deadline, which (because it might reflect real obligations) would be used, as hours ticked away, to extract concessions in return for helping respect it, he preferred to have no sched-ule at all, so that the other side was face-to-face with the dull prospect of his insisting on every point however long it took to resolve it, at the cost to his adversary, unless he compromised his position, of fatigue or hunger, if a mere workday was involved, or larger disruptions in work or fam-ily plans. But this time the impending holiday weekend had made everyone eager for a prompt resolution, and he, for once, really had no program. Nothing required his presence in New York. He had shrunk from planning a vacation—in part because any vacation would have entailed either includ-ing Marie-France, who had declared herself willing to aban-don her share of a Westhampton beach house so that she might join him, or explaining why she was rejected, and in part because the paralyzing nervousness that had overcome him earlier in his room was now recurring whenever he was not occupied with work. He wondered whether he had enough stamina to endure idleness. The more immediate question, however, was what to do that very evening.

At the restaurant table, on the back of yet another piece of promotional cardboard, recommending regional dishes and wines to be tasted that week, he made one of his lists. An eminent Geneva lawyer, Professor Pictet, had been brought by Phil Norris into the last two days of meetings, seemingly as an afterthought, to advise on Swiss procedural law that might apply to the settlement. To everyone's relief, its application could be avoided. The great expert—a man of confident physical vitality, as befitted his rank of colonel in the Swiss army, and of distinguished manners—had taken the opportunity to be especially courteous to Ben, whether out of genuine sympathy, or because he recognized in Ben a source of future retainers, was not clear. Hearing that Ben, unlike the others, was not leaving Geneva, Pictet at once invited him to dinner. On the instant fearful of being cornered, not certain of his mood, Ben had temporized. It would be necessary to telephone with an answer before the nap. He put Pictet at the head of the list; was it a welcome or an unwelcome coincidence that, like the pastor who was Jacques de Todi's father, Professor Pictet resided on the route de Cologny? Would his property also stretch to the highway, stop to permit the rush of traffic to and from Lausanne, and then, on the other side, meander down to the lake, to a private landing marked with a lantern? In Jouve's book there was no description that Ben could remember of the mother. Madame Pictet, in the picture the professor had in his office, was small, plump, and shy, surrounded by three daughters wearing glasses; surprising looks for a Swiss *grande bourgeoise*, different from the towering, blond figure one would have imagined as the consort of a lawyer bearing the name of a venerable Geneva bank or the wife of a great Calvinist divine.

Perhaps because Banque Pictet brought them to mind, next on the list appear the names of two Geneva bankers whom Ben had seen frequently in Paris, bracketed, with the words "I WILL NOT SERVE" next to them. In the context I take this to be Ben's rejection of the passing thought that he might, having just brought to completion a project, immediately, on his own initiative, sustain the boredom of a business dinner. It shows how Ben's irritating habit of expressing himself through pointless allusions persisted. I suppose (but one is at the mercy of the limits of one's own memory and gift for free association) that he had in mind both Leporello and Stephen Dedalus. After the second name there is an asterisk. The related footnote reads: "This man is to be avoided in his domestic setting. Countess [the banker is an Austrian count] is all teeth and knees." Ben concluded the list with the name of a Swissair stewardess, her telephone number, the words "red hair, lips like peeled shrimp, rest unknown, promised to call," and three asterisks. Indeed, it is to her that he attempted to telephone before resting, but he reached instead her roommate, Swiss German, he thought, unable to inform him when Sophie might be at home. Something both eager and falsely girlish in her voice warned Ben that she would flirt with the headwaiter, complain about the asparagus, and expect him to order crepes suzette and coax her into eating them. He decided not to venture the suggestion that she take Sophie's place that evening.

It grew dark. He tried Sophie's number once again, thinking that, after all, he would ask the roommate to have dinner. What business of his were her manners? If she was the tart he imagined, that was just fine as well; copulating until exhaustion with a slut might drain him of the trembling disquiet investing his arms, legs, and sides—all of him, it seemed—until, like Malte's dropsical chamberlain, he could find no rest. This time there was no answer. He composed the number once more, fearing that he had misdialed, and let the ring go on so long that even if she were under the shower washing her hair she must answer. Nothing.

He poured a large brandy, drank it, and called me in Vermont. It had occurred to him that he could ask to stay with us a week or even slightly longer and not call it a vacation; the question of what to do about Marie-France would not arise. He got Prudence's cousin Sean. Sean was staying in our house with his wife and children, while Prudence, the girls, and I, having picked up his boat in Camden, were beating our way south to Nantucket. We intended to sail lazily in those sunny and protected waters, stopping for a hot shower and a shore meal with friends on Nantucket, Martha's Vineyard, and Naushon, until it was time to deliver the boat in New Bedford to a lawyer from Boston who had chartered her for the first two weeks of September.

Ben and Sean knew each other. They had been in the same class in college, had taken some of the same courses. Sean had seemed to Ben, until his senior year, by which time

Rachel's efforts had fitted him with new glasses through which to observe such matters, the epitome of what one would have wished to be—a golden-haired undergraduate with a smooth, smiling face, and clothes, perhaps handed down by a father, evocative of ineffably easy manners, who would greet Ben on Mount Auburn or Dunster Street without slowing his graceful, loping stride and disappear behind the brightly painted door of a final club. At night, when no one would see him, Ben examined those doors with their burnished brass doorknobs and plaques and reflected on the decisiveness with which he had been relegated to a sphere so different from Sean's. The rarefied area of being that lay beyond was impenetrable; he would never apprehend the nature of the mysteries from which he had been excluded, let alone experience them. Indeed, it seemed honorable to refrain from pronouncing the names of those august retreats reserved by Sean and his likes themselves—to feign momentary distraction if another pronounced them, as a Hindu of the shopkeeper caste would take care not to step on the shadow of a Brahman.

Thus Ben's marvel at the transformation Time and Fortune conjoined had wrought in him and Sean was considerable. That the golden, smiling youth should have grown heavy and assumed the comically serious costume and demeanor appropriate to the successful Boston insurance executive he had become was not surprising, but Ben claimed to be astonished that Sean now looked up to him and tried to puzzle out the secrets of his, Ben's, existence. It did not astonish me. Believing without reserve in the world of finance he inhabited, Sean valued like a true connoisseur the extent of Ben's success, and it was now he who wished to penetrate the mysteries of Ben's sphere, whereas for Ben the charm of Sean's secrets had dissipated utterly, like perfume from a bottle left without a stopper. Still, when Sean with his instinctive hospitality, having listened to the reason for Ben's telephone call, urged him to come at once to Vermont and stay as long as he wished, assuring him that he would be as welcome as with Prudence and me, and join in the family's activities or organize his life otherwise in any way he preferred, Ben declined wistfully, explaining with great politeness that the idea of rushing to Vermont from Switzerland on the most crowded weekend of the summer had come as a mad impulse best to be disregarded.

More telephone calls followed. Rebecca was hiking in the Dolomites without an itinerary and would not have an address until the following week; he learned this from Sarah who talked to him more freely than usual. He guessed correctly that she was alone in the house, the professor and his children having driven to Atlantic City, where his parents had retired. He was blue and at loose ends, Ben told Sarah: fit punishment for too much professional success. As soon as the concert was over, while some people in the audience were still applauding, most of the others had shuffled out of the hall to catch the first wave of cruising taxis; the musicians all had wives waiting for them in the suburbs; only the maestro was left quite alone, no one had given a thought to where he might have his dinner. Was the professor going to be away long enough for her to contemplate meeting Ben, for instance in London? They would see some plays, go to the National Gallery, and drink Pimm's cups at the Connaught. It would be a well-deserved vacation for her and a tremendous boost for his morale. He put it all nicely, she has told me, without making her feel any pressure or the sting of his usual sarcasm, so that almost right away she was sorry when she replied that his offer was kind but came too late, the life she had chosen didn't happen to include weekend trips abroad or his grand restaurants and fancy hotels or any of the sort of amusements he was so good at organizing.

But that, after all, is the reality, she said. It's too bad you can't accept it or get out of your jet-set rut. Try Mom, she added. Horace Jones has just walked out on her; she'll probably jump at the chance to have a free trip to London with you.

Curiously, Ben made no mention of this suggestion when he dictated late that night into the portable recorder he had borrowed from Phil Norris. He simply recounted having found Rachel at home, on the North Shore of Boston. She came to the telephone after a long delay, out of breath; the cook, impressed by Ben's calling from Europe and apparently of the view that it was more economical for him to wait than to call again later, had insisted on getting Rachel from the strip of beach at the end of the lawn. It was long enough after lunch, and besides she had been swimming, Ben observed, for the gin and tonics to have worn off. Nonetheless, she was pleasant from the start and seemed appropriately impressed when he explained what he had been doing in Geneva. My, my, my—repeated many times over, for that was how she was in the habit of expressing approval—accompanied his account. That Phil Norris had actually been working for Ben increased her enjoyment; she had memories of him as a dashing veteran at Harvard. Ben told her that having no dinner companion lined up had made him consider eating in his room: possibly a chicken sandwich accompanied by a very large, very cold scotch and soda. He asked if she remembered the wide-ranging comparative study they had made of the quality of such sandwiches—focused on the absolute absence of gristle from the meat and the firmness of the white bread—and how the Boston Ritz had hung on to a narrow lead. She replied in kind. Had they not also zealously studied the speed with which chasseurs in an establishment of the palace category removed cigarette ashes and butts from the cylinders guarding elevator doors and restored their sand to pristine whiteness, the vocabulary the concierge used responding to questions about the hotel's hairdresser, and the relative stiffness of its linen sheets? Ben's heart beat. Suppose he did ask and she consented? He would show her the progress he had made in all areas of instruction, demonstrate the man he had become. But what would happen after the weekend or the week spent together? "Nothing can be whole or sole that has not been rent." It occurred to him that Yeats had written nonsense. The reality was drearily different. He thanked Rachel for talking to a distraught man.

He had been on the telephone so long that the air had turned cold. He closed the windows and drank another brandy to quiet the tingling in his skin—or was his skin actually quivering, although the hand in which he held his glass was steady? He looked at the Rhône, now black and shiny. Beyond lay Calvin's city: in the day green with the lushness of trees, an atmosphere clear and profound, Jouve had written, the most austere in Europe. Was this, too, lyrical nonsense? Had the desperate souls plotting redemption and destruction migrated to other havens? Secret and tortured vices, so Ben had been told, thrived here on the compost of puritanism. He felt again the urgent need of a woman—a woman of low life, degraded, skillful, and unquestioning. These should abound in Geneva; the trick was to find one. Why had there not been a Carvalho among all the Belgians and Japanese to reward the good work he had done? On his own, during walks in the old town, he had already identified certain promising bars: they opened late; some seemed to be above street level. He dressed rapidly, counted the cash in his wallet, and left the hotel, the door key in his pocket. It was better to be able to walk rapidly past the concierge.

The river was very noisy. He walked toward the Grand'Rue, then in the direction of Calvin's church. Each woman out at this hour might be for sale. He had no experience of Geneva's streetwalkers. Did they wait at street corners on heels like stilts, their skirts a mere loincloth, or was the password given by signs of a subtlety worthy of this city, so that the demeanor and garb of a young mother signaled for the connoisseur the nature of her corruption as surely as a colored tag stuck into Camembert told a good housewife that it was ripe to serve that evening? He stopped before café windows, peering attentively inside, looking for women sitting at tables alone, scrutinizing them brazenly. There was no response. Like the old couples beside them, they masticated peaceably and heedlessly or sipped white wine out of little glasses. The bars he had fixed in his memory were dark and very crowded with men. He felt tired. The hotel restaurant would be closed; at the corner of the place du

Bourg-du-Four he found a brasserie that was still serving and ate his dinner at a tiny table alongside two tables of Americans on a bus tour. In the roar of voices he made out the conversation of two women, perhaps his age, perhaps just past it; they had cheerful, ruddy faces and the sort of blouses with little forget-me-nots or plum flowers one would find in the Lord & Taylor's in a wealthy suburb. They were wondering if he spoke English and, if he did, how to go about asking him to join the group for the rest of the evening. He smiled at them. Immediately, they smiled back. As they both were at the edge of the table, facing each other, he found it easy to examine their legs. He saw calves, prickly if he judged correctly and covered by large freckles, flat sandals of brown leather, possibly acquired on a Greek island, toes with unkempt, unlacquered nails. Nostalgia and aversion. He smiled again warmly and walked out of the restaurant.

As he reentered the hall of his hotel, he thought of having recourse to the normal solution for evenings of such wretched loneliness: he could press into the hand of the concierge a folded bank note of large denomination and ask distractedly, perhaps looking away, to have a nice young person directed to his room as soon as that could be arranged. But speaking with the concierge was the female clerk whose task it was to admit clients to their safe-deposit boxes; no guest needing her services, who might cause her to return to her desk, was in sight. Besides, the concierge's face lacked ruse and servility. Would he decline the service, Ben asked himself, and, if so, how was Ben going to avoid him for the balance of his stay and when someday he returned to the hotel? How long was he going to remain in Geneva? Would he ever come back?

These questions couldn't be answered. He stopped at the entrance of the bar. No single women, only couples and men drinking together.

Pages dated "Night of 11/8/71":

> Took 2 Seconals and drank brandy. Got the waiter to bring a bottle so I needn't keep ringing—besides, room service must stop at some hour, even here. Nothing doing; can't sleep. Masturbated carefully, so as not to stain bathrobe, and then ate a chocolate bar. *Niente* sleep. Three in the morning. I communed with Norris's machine again until the tape ran out. Must buy some tomorrow if such a thing exists in Geneva. Poor Jack. What's the point of these outpourings or of scribbling away as I do now except I am so frighteningly awake and reading makes me even more nervous? Twitch twitch.
>
> Preposterous, vehement urge to call Véronique in Saint-Jean-de-Luz. Disguise my voice, say I raise funds for Vassar or want to confirm her bank balance. This gets her to the telephone. Better yet, keep calling until finally it is she who answers. Will she go to some place where we can speak: the post office, the Miramar? In the dark of the booth, hearing me plead, she relents. Then, I go to Biarritz. Enact the dream of last August. Hôtel du Palais, white room, arms and limbs entwined, cooled by the ocean breeze. We efface the images of this year.
>
> It will not be. I was unable to seize what she once

offered with such keen ardor and now there is
nothing to retract, nothing to forgive, nothing to take.

During my last visit here, I crossed the river on the
Pont des Bergues, doubled back, and near the place
de la Fusterie noticed in a store window a sweater—
red bordering on orange—like none I had seen
before.

I go in. Walls done in some dark wood and tall
mirrors. I am the sole client. A profusion of
merchandise of unique quality and exorbitant cost
surrounds me. Spread on counters, draped on tailors'
dummies, are clothes for men accustomed only to silk
and cashmere, full-fashioned and ample on their
bodies. Their feet, encased in slippers of soft leather,
sink in rich carpets. How has my life brought me to
this place? I think of mother cursing my father's
ledgers, an abyss opening at the end of each month.
Undeterred, I ask for the sweater. A tall man, with
the voice of a "better person," as my mother would
have said, brings it to me. It is single-ply cashmere;
he recommends it for summer evenings, but finds me
hard to fit. My shoulders do not balance the incipient
thickness in the waist. All this he tells me with the
greatest kindness, and at last finds a solution: I will
have a sleeveless model (thus eliminating the
complication posed by the length of sleeves); there is
one in my color in a size that will be just right. My
father preferred sweaters without sleeves, considering
that they were more comfortable under a suit coat.

Perhaps for that reason, ever since such things have
been within my control, I have only sweaters with
sleeves and deprecate men who wear any sort of
sweater at all with their suit. All this, on an impulse, I
divulge to the salesman. He claims to understand me
perfectly: how one dresses is a matter of such very
personal feelings. Then Monsieur Motte (by this time
I know his name) shows me an overcoat of black
cashmere—generous, light, and, he assures me,
particularly warm. He promises I will not feel the bise
on the Pont de la Machine even in the dead of winter.
What can I say? I buy the sweater and the
overcoat—sending the latter to New York—pay the
stupendous price in specie so as to rise higher yet in
Monsieur Motte's esteem and direct my steps to the
Hôtel des Bergues, crossing this time on the bridge
where my new garment is to be of such succor.

The water is of an extreme limpidity until,
approaching the herse that guards the machine, it
becomes an opaque hell boiling so violently that I
draw back from the parapet. I reflect on my quite
unneeded new coat and how readily I have bought it
to please the courteous salesman who knew how to
flatter solemnly and amuse. A poor person would find
it far more difficult—perhaps impossible—to extract
from me such a sum.

A day or two before I first heard Véronique's name
mentioned, in Jack's presence, I told Prudence a
gratuitous lie: I pretended I didn't know why in
France Indian summer is called *l'été de la Saint-*

Martin. There was no going back on falsehood; how could I explain anything so grotesque? But to me it was clear why I had lied, and I wondered whether Jack, who kept so quiet, understood as well: it is that I am without charity (therefore without love) and full of envy. On that hill above a vineyard, my friend and his wife united since so long ago by such affection, I could not bear to tell the story of the man who gave his coat to a beggar.

After that terrible night—two more Seconals eventually brought Ben sleep—he went out to run his errands. The light was intolerably bright. In a shop next door to the hotel he found, among watches, Swiss army knives, and wood carvings, dark glasses in an imitation tortoiseshell frame. He bought these. So screened, he turned away from the river and stopped at the cigar store. He intended to buy only four of the Montecristos with little tails that reminded him of the three little pigs and that he liked for those tails as much as for their taste and slender form. He had calculated that, considering the plans he was making, this was the number he needed, but his acquaintance, the elderly lady in charge of the humidor whose tirades against Davidoff had formed a bond between them, seemed surprised, so he quickly excused himself and confirmed that indeed he would take his usual box of Especials. The pharmacy was on the other side of the street, at the end. Ben knew that it too was an establishment directed by women. He entered, removed his dark glasses, and explained to the youngest of them that, doubtless because of the rough handling of luggage at the airport, the tops of the bottles of his sleeping pills and hay-fever pills had come off in his toilet kit, that apparently his shaving lotion had leaked, and he was faced with leaving in the afternoon for Morocco—where he would remain until the end of the month—with soggy paste in place of the medication he badly needed. He showed her the bottle of Seconal and the dismal traces of the accident and offered to pay for a telephone call to the doctor in New York whose name appeared on the label. The white-coated figures consulted. His interlocutor returned and asked where he was staying. He told her, adding that he was well known at the hotel, and volunteered to let her see his passport. That turned out to be unnecessary. She would be pleased to sell him thirty Seconals (the number noted on the tube he had shown her) and as many tablets of a Swiss antihistamine closely resembling the one to which he was accustomed, to use as needed. He thanked her and asked about Dictaphone tape. That could be purchased a few storefronts away, in the direction of the quai des Bergues.

A sense of elation that had the taste of tears overcame Ben. His charms were working. What remained to be done was easy and restful. In his hotel bathroom, there were twenty-six Seconals in a box to which he had transferred them. He had at least that many tranquilizers. If he took the lot with a bottle of burgundy, having first given orders not to be disturbed for any reason, there was no chance of failure. At the concierge's desk he opened the Montecristo box, took out a cigar and lit it, then asked that the package be put in his room, and walking, contrary to habit, very slowly, since it was hot and he wanted to enjoy the cigar, made his way down to the park known as the Promenade de la Treille, which slopes steeply below the Hôtel de Ville.

In the shade, seated on a bench, regretting that he had not brought another Especial, he watched the children and their nursemaids. Swings, red and white rubber balls, sandbox toys, children's hair, the starched striped uniforms—were they all so heartbreakingly fresh because of a special property of the light, now that he had taken off his sunglasses; because the mild hangover from which he still suffered had made the scene mysteriously distant; or because he was having a last look? He remembered the boat pond in the Luxembourg Garden, and certain winter and early spring Sunday mornings at the Ninety-sixth Street playground when, aching from scotch whiskey and wine, and not sleeping pills, he had watched the twins ride their tricycles round and round the jungle gym. He knew most of the mothers on the other benches and the occasional au pair who consented to work on a weekend. Fathers came infrequently, except perhaps after church as part of a family outing. Lawyers and bankers, were they at the office, perfecting yet another draft of an indenture? Was their hangover more severe than Ben's, or were they engaged in male rites of such high solemnity that their good spouses (for that was how they affected to call them), more reverential than Rachel—but he, Ben, in any case knew no rites for that day or any other—had tiptoed away with little Christopher, Kate, and Marian, enjoining them not to disturb Papa? An exception was a man whom Ben knew and felt disliked by, so that they never shared a bench: tall and very thin, sharp legs in well-pressed suit trousers, hat with a high crown and a tiny feather on his balding head, he read the Sunday *Times* from the beginning to end, refolding each section carefully, while his twin boys clad in green snowsuits tormented Sarah and Rebecca. The memory was unconnected to the present scene except by the azure of the sky; could it be that the winter sky in New York had the same acute purity? Whatever the answer, Ben began to cry and hastily retreated. It occurred to him that he would walk along the Corraterie, where Jouve had placed the bank for which Baladine worked, and so he returned to the hotel, crossing the Rhône over the Pont de l'Île.

It was midafternoon by then. He ordered a chicken sandwich and white wine to be served in his room, cried again until abruptly all self-pity left him, finished lunch, and dictated to the end of the tape he had bought. And—with the exception of the note I mention below—that account is the last to have come from Ben. The rest I learned the following week, having arrived in Geneva from Edgartown, on Martha's Vineyard, where I left Sean's boat, Prudence, and the girls. The Swiss police had summoned me; I was named as next of kin in a note on the desk of the hotel room.

Ben was dead, of course, but not according to plan. Apparently, instead of taking a short nap when he had finished lunch and exhausted his new tape (he wanted to experience once more the joy of innocent sleep), and then dining lightly, again in his room—after which he intended to down the pills with a bottle of Vosné-Romanée—he fell into a torpor so profound, probably induced by a few Seconals he had taken to make sure that sleep did not elude him, that, when he next called room service, it was to ask for the following morning's breakfast. Between that time and the moment, some hours later, at which he left the hotel, he must have written the words "I will end it this morning" on that sheet of letter paper dated August 13, which the police found together with my name and telephone number. The day concierge remembered greeting him and noticing that he was wearing dark glasses. Two English couples on holiday, who happened to be on the Pont de la Machine, observed a well-dressed and very pale man, with such glasses, bent over the parapet, as though he were studying the turbulence below. Moments later, with what they described as astonishing agility, the man had climbed on the parapet and executed a beautiful dive, arms opening seconds before he hit the water. It was they who called the police and waited, in a crowd that quickly gathered, for the team that removed Ben's body from the teeth of the great herse.

A NOTE ON THE TYPE

This book was set in Fournier, a typeface named for Pierre Simon Fournier *fils* (1712–1768), a celebrated French type designer. Coming from a family of typefounders, Fournier was an extraordinarily prolific designer of typefaces and of typographic ornaments. He was also the author of the important *Manuel Typographique* (1764–1766), in which he attempted to work out the system standardizing type measurement in points, a system still in use internationally.

Fournier's type is considered transitional in that it drew its inspiration from the old style, yet was ingeniously innovational, providing for an elegant yet legible appearance. In 1925 his type was revived by the Monotype Corporation of London.

Composed by Crane Typesetting Service, Inc., West Barnstable, Massachusetts.

Designed by Peter A. Andersen